Gerry Byrne lives in London, where she
works in a women's hostel in Soho. *Ruby*
is her first novel.

GERRY BYRNE

RUBY

VISTA

First published in Great Britain 1996
by Victor Gollancz

This Vista edition published 1997
Vista is an imprint of the Cassell Group
Wellington House, 125 Strand, London WC2R 0BB

© Gerry Byrne 1996

A catalogue record for this book is
available from the British Library.

ISBN 0 575 60233 3

Printed and bound in Great Britain by
Caledonian International Book Manufacturing Ltd,
Glasgow

97 98 99   10 9 8 7 6 5 4 3 2 1

the world soon kills

I have always been drawn to watching people destroy themselves. If enough others go first, maybe my turn won't come.

I am standing in a high place, the horizon far below me. My arm rests on grey stone.

It is my job to watch. Watch them falling like dolls, over and over. Over and over, down to a whispering tissue-paper sea. My hand holds tight to the stone rail. The waist-high parapet. Cold stone my waist, my belly.

I lean. Over and over. Watch the falling dolls. One and another. Over the whispering paper. Ocean as grey as ribbons. I freeze tight to stone. Reaching.

The boy leached grey as paper. Rolls over and over. Waving like ribbons, weightless. It is my job to watch, not catch. Slow as dolls they go over. Reaching like ribbons.

Cold stone my belly.

Over and over.

I dream this.

Over and over.

'It is in the blood.'

the smallest office in the world

That first day I polished the little brass plate. Lovingly traced the capital A. 'Haydon Aachen Consultancy'. Beautiful. Goodbye, welfare state, hello, enterprise culture.

Names are funny things. Evian got hers from a water bottle. 'Aachen' I got from my grandmother. I thought it would give me priority in the Business Pages. Just behind Triple A. Wrong. I ended up stuffed among the Hs. 'Haydon', that's another story.

I looked at my bronzed reflection. Short dark hair, yellow eyes, strong jaw. A big strong woman, but light on my feet. I tripped up the stairs, keys at the ready.

When I saw Evian swinging her long legs on my new desk in my virginal office I wanted to say something wounding. 'Get your big hairy legs off my desk. However much you shave, the stubble always shows. Men's hair is just so much coarser.'

I didn't say it. Evian and I go back a long way and we share a guilty secret.

'Evian,' (she pronounces it like an endless '*deviant*' so I follow suit), 'why do you have to wreck my first day?'

'Cup of tea, *chérie*?'

She's being French: it's a bad sign. 'No, I won't lend you any money. I object to financing your habit. Besides I've sunk every last *sou* into this place. Which, I may point out, you have illegally entered.'

'God, you're touchy this morning. Got kicked out of the wrong side of the bed? Oh no, I forgot, you don't. Mardy old spinster.'

'Evian, please, you know I can't abide canny Northern talk first thing in the morning. Thee may do that kind o' t'thing in Buggeritt, but it won't wash down here.'

Buggeritt was the mythical birthplace of Evian, then called Steven, a mining village on the Notts/Yorkshire borders 'where men were men and there was nowt else woth takking of'. Which was why Steven came down here, and became Evian.

She stuck down the end of an eyelash that was threatening to uncurl. 'What's with this consultancy, then?'

'I'm getting too old for the frontline stuff. I thought I'd start my own business.'

'Thee privatized? Never thought I'd see the day. What are you going to do? Scoop us degenerates off the street and turn us in for bounty?'

'Nothing as hands-on as that. Training, team-building, personal effectiveness, that's what I'm offering.'

She looked at me narrowly. 'Eh? You just said all them words and I still don't know what you're on about.'

I thought I might as well practise my sales pitch on her. 'Well,' I said, fixing her with my best businesswoman direct look, 'the skills I have developed in personal social work management are readily transferable. I'm . . . Oh, for God's sake, Evian. Management consultancies are about the only growth area in this recession. And I'm sick of the mess and blood of other people's lives. It's this or burn-out.'

She gazed at her fingernails and tossed back her tall hair. 'You don't seem to be overrun with business.'

'It's my first day.'

'You need help. An office has to have help. Any proper office.'

'Can you type?'

She batted her fur-lined eyes back as if I'd asked about her skills in tight-rope walking.

'Filing?'

She tottered round the desk in five-inch heels with an envelope in her hands.

'That's not filing. Filing is putting things in order so they're easy to locate.'

She sighed and swung back on to the corner of the desk. 'Have you finished? Right, *chérie*, I will tell you what I had in mind.'

'I can't wait to hear.'

She placed one long-nailed hand over her crossed knee. 'I'm not prepared to ruin my nails on a typewriter. The only filing I do is on these.' They were painted pale coral with white moons and tips. 'Do you know how many hours these take?'

I shook my head and shrugged.

'Your problem is you don't appreciate appearances. I know you think you're better than other people because you've got no vices but it doesn't work like that.'

I opened my mouth to protest that I did have vices; I just didn't indulge them in doorways off Shaftesbury Avenue.

She silenced me with a wave of coral.

'Appearances matter. People see your flat shoes and your sensible jumble-sale cardies and they draw conclusions.'

I hugged my second-hand cashmere and glared at her.

'You want an office in the West End? You need staff. You need a receptionist, someone to answer the telephone, someone to keep the visitors entertained while you're busy with your clients . . .'

'Evian, look around. One desk, one lock-up cupboard, a filing cabinet, a chair. There's no room for anything else.'

She dropped her eyes like an interval curtain. When the silence was sufficiently deep, she said, 'You still haven't got it. How are you going to drum up business?'

'Evian, get out. I am not interested in your kind of business. I don't want you leaning into car windows purring, "Haydon Aachen Consultancy, first floor on the left." Go. Now. Leave my premises.'

She slid off the desk, pulled her tiny skirt down over her stocking tops. She squinted down at me through her top lashes. 'You'll regret it. Treating me like a two-bit whore.'

I couldn't resist a parting crack. 'How are you earning your money, then?'

'Clipping.' She opened the door. 'Round the clubs.' She shut the door with a smart click of the new lock.

I had to chase down the stairs after her. 'Evian, come back. Let's talk. I'll have to report it.' Old habits . . .

She stopped. 'It's not your business any more. You've got this.' She waved her hand to include the whole block.

'Wish I did. Evian, it's not my job any more, but I worry about you. Clipping's dangerous.'

'Safer than some. There's no exchange of body fluids.'

I winced as she knew I would. 'That's not the only risk you run. Punters pay for something and you don't deliver, they can get angry. You could get killed.'

She shrugged. 'I'm not stupid. I take care of myself.'

She slid down on to the third step. I suddenly noticed how tired she looked.

'Is that what you call it? Taking care of yourself?'

She sighed, then grinned. 'You're not so bad, Hallie. I don't want paying, all I want is a key.'

'The locks didn't stop you this time.'

'You're going to change them tomorrow. You're soft, but you're not that soft.'

'I'll think about it, Evian. Take care, love. Don't get yourself killed. Life would be very dull without you.'

'*Au revoir, chérie.*'

I wasn't really surprised, as I passed the postman on the stairs next morning, at the throaty call from above my head. Evian was standing outside my office with my post pincered between her painted fingers. Magenta they were today.

'What time do you call this, then?' She dropped the three letters into my hand and ostentatiously consulted her watch.

'Sorry,' I cried. 'I didn't realize I'd employed you as my overseer. Still, you do have a lot of experience of cracking whips.'

She rolled her eyes. 'It doesn't make a good impression, you know.'

I busied myself with the new hefty double locks. 'I'm glad to see these kept you out.'

'Possibly. You're changing the subject. You're late at the office and you've created a very poor impression on a potential client.'

'The tube was stuck for ages in a tunnel at Kennington. What potential client?'

'Public transport? If you must use it don't advertise the fact. The Northern line!' The magenta lips puckered as if they'd bitten on an unripe plum. 'How unutterably tacky.'

'What potential client? What did you say to them?'

She tossed her head slightly and ran her fingers down her body as if dusting off an invisible cloak. '*Voilà.*'

I dropped my head on to the desk. 'Get out, Evian.'

She gathered herself up slowly. At the door she turned. 'I wouldn't bet on the locks.'

'What?'

'Since I came as a client, I thought it would be bad manners to break in. Don't be fooled by the thick brass; that's just decoration. It wouldn't stop a determined operator.'

I banged my forehead on the desk. 'Evian, what are you trying to do to me?'

'Ah, *chou-chou*, don't cry. I just found you a bit of work so you wouldn't starve to death in this pretty little office.'

'I've got work, Evian. I wouldn't have started out if I didn't have enough work for three months. The training resources pack will see me through any slack periods.'

'But this is much more interesting.'

'OK.' I sighed. 'What is it?'

'A missing person.'

'Go to the police.'

She slid back on to the desk. From between her breasts she retrieved a small navy chamois-leather pouch. 'This is your payment if you find her.'

I held up my hand to stop her before she could undo the drawstring. 'No, Evian. No.'

'What do you mean no? Costs nowt to look.'

'Evian, don't open the bag. I can't afford to have knock-off gear on my premises.'

'Do you think I'm stupid? It's legit. I was given it by her friend. So as to locate the owner.'

'You've got proof it's not stolen?'

'Could get it easy enough.'

'Why can't you go to the police?'

She stood, snatched up the bag. 'Might have known you'd take their side against a poor working girl with no friends in high places.'

'Give over, Evian. I've heard it too often.'

'I suppose you'll be pleased when you hear she's dead.'

I ignored her and turned my attention to the post. A business-machines exhibition, cut-price tickets; the local directory – would I like to pay for an entry? How did I get on their mailing lists so quickly? Ah, the women's housing co-operative. Looked like they'd finally made up their minds. 'Shit! Stupid cows.'

'Language, *chérie*.' I'd forgotten she was still there.

'It's this bloody housing project. They've been dangling this work in front of me for months. Just one more committee. I was going to start next week. I can't believe they're doing this to me.'

'Can't you sue them?'

'Nothing in writing.'

She flipped open her compact and began reapplying lip-liner. 'So you've got a little window in your schedule, after all?'

'All right, what's the story? Who's dead?'

'Rusty has gone missing. Ruby Tuesday, whatever she's calling herself. She left the Paradise Now club just after midnight on Friday. She was due on for her last act at one a.m. It was just a meal break. She never returned.'

'People do disappear, Evian. She might have been trying to avoid someone.'

'Chantal doesn't think so.'

'Who's Chantal?'

chantal

I climbed the creaking stairs with several thousand pounds'
worth of antique ruby ring in my pocket. I'm not normally
so reckless but it seemed important to have something of
Rusty's.

The lino in the centre of the treads was worn away to
reveal the wood beneath. At the edges, thick slopes of black
waxy deposits leered at me. It was just a few streets away
from my neat office.

She'd said not before eleven. She worked late. It was
nearer noon. Even so, there was a long wait, groaned curses
and the scrabbling of sheets before she let me in.

The curtains were closed and Chantal turned on the
unshaded centre light. Its glare bleached the life from her
face. Her lank half-permed hair was the colour and texture
of bladderwrack, her lipstick the brown of dried blood. Her
eyes were hollows of old mascara and kohl pencil. She had
the pale helpless look of the newly woken. In another light
she might have been beautiful.

I smiled. 'It's very good of you to see me.'

She shrugged and nodded me to an old settee. The dust
rose when I sat on it. The room smelled of incense and dirty
underwear.

'Tell me about Rusty.'

'What's to tell? We been here three years. She never, you
know, gone off without telling me before. Coffee?'

I nodded.

Chantal fetched me a cup of something black and bitter.

'Did she have punters here?' I asked. 'Or take them somewhere else.'

'She weren't on the game.' Her look said she wished it were cyanide she was spooning into my coffee.

'But she went with men for money?'

'Not like you mean.'

'You tell me, then. Where did she get the jewellery, this ring?' I held it between thumb and forefinger. Its light stained my fingers like a birthmark. 'I don't know much, but I know you don't earn money like that as a dancer.'

Her eyes narrowed. There were little flakes of mascara spotting the grey beneath. 'You don't earn money like that on the streets either, sweetheart,' she spat.

'So?' I held the ring out to her.

'Some john gave it to her. That was his name, John. Good joke, eh?'

'So a man called John gave her a three-thousand-pound ruby. You explain to me what that was for.'

'Said it was for security. Like, if anything happened to him. Older than her, see. He was her friend.'

'Lover?'

She sniffed. 'She said I should have it. To remember her, like. I got to go out soon. Have you finished asking me questions?'

Too close to the mark, eh? I said, 'Look, Chantal, if you want me to find her, you've got to give me something to go on. Do you think she might have gone off with this John?'

She just looked at me.

'Well, isn't it possible?'

'No!' The corners of her mouth were beginning to twitch. 'She wouldn't.'

'You don't know that she didn't?' I dropped the ring back into its pouch.

She pulled handfuls of hair and shook her head mutely.

'Well? Why wouldn't she?'

She sighed. 'You don't know fuck all, do you?'

I spread my hands. 'Enlighten me.'

'Men like him don't set up home with the likes of us, only in stories. Besides, he's already married.'

'Who said anything about marriage?'

'She's not stupid, you know.'

'I never said she was.'

'She's got a nice little set-up here with me. She wouldn't go and spoil it. She would have wanted marriage or nothing.'

'Just an old-fashioned girl?' I put the ring away.

'You want to see her things?'

I thought I might as well. I wasn't getting very far with the questions.

Chantal opened Rusty's wardrobe. 'See, all her clothes are here. She wasn't going anywhere.'

All her clothes. I wanted to cry when I looked at them. Lots of black. Short dresses and skirts. Some leggings, black jeans and slacks. A couple of best blouses. Lots of belts, red, black, white, thick, thin, brass-buckled, studded, chain-link, gold. All her clothes and not one that told me anything about Rusty. Who was she? I closed the door.

'What was she wearing?'

'Her dancing clothes. And a dark blue mac. Let me think, what was the last club she was doing? Pink Flamingo?'

'No, that's not the one Evian mentioned.'

'Anyway.' She opened another cupboard. 'Be able to work it out from here.'

The smell brought me back to riding lessons when I was

a teenager. The tack room. It wasn't so different. The leather had the black shine of work and sweat. The brass was dulled the same way. This wasn't the gleaming horse gear hung from olde oake rafters in countrified pubs. This was the real thing. Work harness. There were other things. Pieces of red net hung with gold coins; sequined chiffon; basques and scraps of lacy lingerie. Mostly it was leather. Leather was Rusty's trademark.

'Not quite the stuff you'd choose to go away in.'

Chantal put her arms round the waist of the red net dress as if it were a fragile dancing partner.

'Thanks,' I said.

'You can take her diaries. There.' She nodded towards a little pile on the dressing-table. She stood with her back to me, still caught up in the dress. 'There's nothing personal in them. But you might get some names.'

I picked up the diaries. They were slim pocket appointments' books, not fat confessional volumes. The last three years, in blue, black and red covers.

As I turned to go I caught sight of a framed photo among the spilled make-up and tissues. It was a grey blurred picture of a young woman and child. The quality of the print didn't match the frame, which looked as expensive as anything in the room. I picked it up.

'Is this Rusty?'

Chantal nodded. 'About ten years ago.'

I couldn't tell much. She'd been a slim, dark-haired girl with a pretty, slightly wan face. She could have changed a lot in those ten years.

'I thought you said she had red hair?' My face in the mirror had gone as grey as the picture.

'Yeah, just looks dark in that photo. Black and white, innit?'

16

Black and white always gets me this way. 'She was a natural redhead? Not dyed?'

'It was natural. I'd know if anyone, wouldn't I?'

'Who's the child?'

'Her son. Kenny, I think his name was.'

She was still talking over her shoulder. I swung her round to face me. 'Chantal, don't you think that's a big thing just to drop casually into the conversation? Don't you want her found?'

She pulled away from me, bared her teeth. 'Fuck off of me arm. She ain't seen him for years. Adopted, in 'e?'

'He still has a right to know if anything's happened to his mother. If only when he's grown-up.'

'Be about twelve now.' She was rocking the red dress in her arms. The last of her mascara rolled down her white cheeks. 'Twelve or thirteen.'

'You do want her found, Chantal?'

'Course I do. I just can't take questions.'

That was all I could get out of her.

dear heart

How do you check out all the Johns in a street girl's diary?

After the first day, I gave up ringing the numbers and asking for John. I thought if I heard, 'We've got dozens of Johns. If you could give the surname . . .' one more time I would set light to the phone. I shouldn't have been surprised that there were so many business numbers, but I was.

A vague pattern was emerging. There were several entries with 'John' and then a phone number in the date part of the diary, as opposed to the addresses at the back. Sometimes the number would be repeated, but several months apart. Either there was more than one John and Rusty saw them on a cyclical basis or, as seemed more likely, one John moved around between business numbers.

There were a couple of exceptions but not enough to alter my next line of attack. I would concentrate on the repeated numbers, phone them up and find out the nature of their business and whether there was anything that connected them together. For that I needed a cover story. I decided on a variant of the truth: I had just started my own management and training consultancy and I'd like some information about their line of business.

After three days I had a great wad of data but no clear idea where to go with it. They were all medium-sized firms, of between twenty and a hundred employees, with products ranging from children's party-bags to scientific textbooks.

18

Four sold financial services. There were two registered charities. I nearly came a cropper there. One of the receptionists had worked with me years ago on a drugs project. 'That you, Hal? God, it's been ages. So you're a training consultant now. Well, well.'

I was glad I hadn't strayed too far into fantasy for my research. It reminded me, though, of the work I was leaving undone to pursue this idiotic chase. I still had to bill the women's housing collective for the work I'd done so far, and there was a conference on new developments in criminal justice.

One more John, I promised myself, then I'll get on with some real work.

'Christine Deerhart.' The voice was ice-cool. It did something peculiar to my stomach. *Carole.*

'Good afternoon, I wonder if you could spare a few moments to answer—' I was having difficulty keeping my voice steady. I was glad I had a written script next to the phone.

'I don't buy over the phone.'

I rushed in before she could put the phone down. 'And I'm not selling. Your business—'

'This is a personal phone. I think you have the wrong number.'

One final try. 'I am sorry. My mistake. This is the number I was given by Hughes and Dolby.' I read the top name off my John list.

She exhaled over the line, half-way between a breath and a laugh. *She used to breathe like that.* 'Ah, a silly mistake. My husband does do work for Hughes and Dolby. They've given you his home number instead of the office. Please hold on one moment and I'll find it for you.' She gave me a number.

'That's John Deerhart?' I checked.

'That's right. Actually today he's at Parrotts'. Would you like that number?'

That was the party-bag place. 'I think I've already got that one. Thank you.' I read it out. Establish my *bona fides*. 'Sorry to have troubled you.'

'Not at all. I apologize for being so brusque earlier. I took you for one of those ghastly telesales persons. Whom shall I say called?'

I gave her my name and number. This looked like the John. A modern marriage. I wasn't sure I could take another one of those. I wondered if Rusty was his only bit of rough. There was something unconvincing about Christine Deerhart. Not quite right. Too helpful. *Or was it just that she sounded so like someone I used to know?* I was glad I wasn't going to meet her. Too many memories to stir up.

I now had another problem. How do you call a man up and ask him about his relationship with a missing stripper?

A little more research revealed: his firm were accountants, which explained why he spent so much time at other people's offices; his home number was a Surrey exchange – my mother was ringing back with the full address from her local phone book; he'd appeared in all three diaries so he must have known Rusty for at least three years; the firm were doing well, judging from their client list, and he was a partner so he can't have been going short.

What would the Great Detective make of this? So, Mr Deerhart, what were you doing with Rusty? Were you responsible for her disappearance? Did you kill her?

I hit on the idea of asking his professional advice about 'payments in kind'. I'd been offered an expensive piece of jewellery and wondered if I had to declare it for tax purposes. He suggested meeting me for lunch when I mentioned a mutual friend – a redhead. He sounded quite pleased to hear from me. Maybe he thought I was another call-girl muscling in on Rusty's pitch.

He said he already had a table booked. 'Do you know the restaurant On Top of the World?'

'No.'

'Where are you coming from? It's—'

'No. I know where it is,' I said. 'I just don't do that.'

'Pardon? You never eat lunch? You could join me for one glass of wine. Or a mineral water.'

I couldn't explain. 'All right, I'll meet you at one.'

My last therapist said I shouldn't force myself to confront my phobias. There would come a point in my life when they would just fall away because I didn't need them. The one before that said the exact opposite.

I'm not afraid of lifts as such. It's just that when the floors go above nine, the numbers start multiplying and playing tricks. I took deep breaths and watched the white triangle slide sideways, counting up. Six. Seven. Eight. 100. 1001. 12002. I close my eyes. A long black shaft stretches away from me. Tapered. Obsidian. A narrow wedge like a railway line pointing off to infinity.

'Restaurant.'

The lobby swam and righted itself. 'I'd like to be seated inside, facing inward.' I added as an afterthought, 'Oh, I'm meeting somebody. He may be here already.'

John Deerhart was younger than I'd expected. He seemed a mild sort of man. At least, he didn't object to my dictating the seating arrangements. His mouse-grey hair, brushed back behind his ears, watery blue eyes and thin features gave him a mournful appearance – except that he had a nervous habit of bunching up his cheeks like a greedy hamster. He was obviously nervous now. He turned the ring round in his long-nailed fingers.

'Yes, I recognize this ring. It came to me from my aunt.' He blinked at me over the cheek-pouches, flinching as if he'd been caught gorging the sunflower seeds.

'Odd thing to leave to a man.'

He shrugged, more like a hiccup. 'I offered it to my wife. She didn't like it – too gaudy.'

'It's a sizeable stone, a real ruby, I had it checked.'

Its light spilled over his fingers like a wine stain. Another convulsive twitch. 'She didn't want it. It didn't go with any of her things.'

I stared at him for a moment, trying to fathom how a woman who turned up her nose at a jewel worth a few grand could end up with this creature. If it wasn't money, it couldn't have been sex, could it? Was there something I was missing?

'But it suited Rusty? It went with her things?' I couldn't keep the sarcasm out of my voice as I thought of the leather underwear and studded collars.

'Red was her colour. I used to call her my flame-haired temptress.'

I dropped my head into my hands. It was true about chartered accountants. I looked up at him. No, there was no trace of irony. But I picked up something else. 'You used the past tense. Do you think she's dead?'

'No, it's just that she's the past for me. We split up. I haven't seen her for months.'

'Why?'

'I told you. We split up. She broke up with me. Said she didn't want to see me any more.'

'Did she give a reason?'

'She said I was boring her.' He raised his blue eyes to meet mine. There were tears in them.

I took the ring back. 'Have you any idea where she could have gone that Friday?'

He shook his head. 'I thought you might have a message from her. That's why I agreed to see you. If you do find anything out, would you tell me? We could meet here next week.'

The 'poor little rich boy' smile made my teeth ache. 'I don't think I'm quite your type.'

'You misunderstand me.' He brushed the thin hair back behind his ears with long fingers. They were quite lovely hands, pale, idle, like a lady's. 'It wasn't like that. Rusty . . . We slept together, of course, but . . . Men don't spend that kind of money on women they don't—'

'Men spend their money on the strangest things,' I said.

He dropped his head into those beautiful hands as if to give me a better view. 'You won't understand.'

'My friends tell me I'm stupid, Mr Deerhart. Frequently. But even I'm not that stupid.'

'You're lucky to have such friends. They are the rarest. That's what I'm trying to tell you about Rusty. She was so straight. She never dressed anything up to spare one's feelings. My wife's like that in her own way. But Rusty, she never lied. So when she said I was b – b – booo—' The rest was lost in his napkin.

I would not sit there while a man cried his eyes out over a tart with a heart of gold. It was too much. 'Chantal said she wanted to get married.'

He nodded. 'She wanted a real family. Whatever that is. It was the one thing I couldn't give her.'

Please. I left him with the bill and a parting question. 'Is that why you killed her?'

It was worth a try. It worked in detective stories.

His face went as white as the starched linen tablecloth.

the boy

'Not in my office. Can't you read?' I pointed to the notice, in elegant brown calligraphy on buff parchment, 'No Exotic Cheroots'.

Evian wobbled her eyes at it. 'Spliffs?' She lit up just the same.

'Please, Evian. I'll have to throw you out. I'm a respectable businesswoman trying to make an honest living. All you've brought me so far is bad luck.'

'All right, *chérie*.' She took two more draws, then carefully put out the cigarette and replaced it in its cardboard tube in a blue tampon-holder in her handbag. 'So you haven't got very far with Rusty?'

'The police were less than helpful. As soon as I said where she was last seen, they just guffawed. Girls like that go missing all the time. Probably hiding from her pimp.'

'She hasn't got a pimp.'

'Just repeating what they said. I don't know where to go from here. I've tried all my contacts in the street agencies. Was she using?'

Evian shook her head. 'Just pills.'

'Pity. What am I saying? I don't mean that. It's just that if she was, she'd have to surface to get her stuff.'

Evian nodded. 'Chantal does, though.' She took out a packet of chewing gum, offered me a stick. 'What did you think to the punter?'

I shook my head to the gum. 'He wouldn't like to be called that. I don't know. He's a strange piece of work but that doesn't mean anything. I might meet him for lunch next week.'

'Rich?' Evian's eyes went unfocused. 'Handsome?'

'If you like that sort of thing.'

'I do, I do,' she purred. 'I think I'll come with you. You don't think he might be one of my . . . ?' She searched for the word.

'Mugs? I'm sure you've got the panache to carry it off.'

She basked her eyelids.

'Remember he's married, Evian.'

'Aren't they all. Children?'

'Don't know. Listen, Evian, you didn't tell me Rusty had a child.'

'Oh, forgot. She never talked about him.'

'That's what Chantal said. I think she's hiding something.'

'She's just upset, had one adopted. Five-year-old. If I got married I'd like to have a child. Adopt one, I mean.'

'Evian!'

'It's natural, wanting to have babies.' She pouted.

'I was wondering whether Rusty might have wanted to find him, her child. She might suddenly have seen him. It happens.'

Evian rolled her eyes. 'In the middle of the night?'

'Maybe she saw a young boy on the streets that reminded her of him. If he was being abducted.'

'You read too many Sunday papers.'

'What do you think's happened to her, then?'

'I think she was picked up in a car. Not a punter, Mr Right, and he says, "I have searched three continents for you and now I have found you," and he takes her back to

25

his mansion and buys her a whole new wardrobe of clothes so she doesn't need the old tat—'

'And what have you been reading?'

'It's better than thinking she was stabbed for her earnings in some back alley.'

'Where's the body?'

'Exactly. They'd have just left her there. Police won't investigate. Just another girl.'

'I'll ask Chantal about the boy.'

I arranged to see Chantal early evening in the White Lion.

Time to check out Rusty's work. I'd put it off for long enough. The Pink Flamingo was first. It gaped, like a missing tooth, between a fast-food bar and a newsagent's, a black hole leading down some dark stairs. A pudding-faced girl in a short black dress and sheer black stockings stood at the top of the stairs. I'd seen a twin of that dress in Rusty's wardrobe. She hopped from one foot to the other as if she had a kidney infection.

'I'd like to speak to the proprietor.'

'Yeah?' She moved something round in her mouth with her tongue.

'The boss. Whoever runs this place.'

She stared at me, then abruptly shouted over her shoulder, 'Jimmie!'

Jimmie bounded up the stairs, a short spotty youth, maybe early twenties, in a striped shirt, braces and gold elasticated sleeve grips. I think he modelled himself on his namesake in the *Superman* comics.

'Yeah?'

'Lady wants to see the boss.'

He pulled his braces. 'What gan I do for you?' The C got lost somewhere around his adenoids.

'Are you the owner?'

He shot a glance at the girl, thought better of lying. 'I manage this glub for Mr Grazeley. Any business to do with here I gan deal with.'

'I'd rather speak to Mr Grazeley. Where can I find him?'

He shrugged. 'One of his other glubs probably.' He sounded like one of the Flowerpot Men. 'Who shall I say was asking?'

I gave him my card. 'He can ring for an appointment.'

Someone had put a lot of thought into the lighting at the White Lion. The interior was passable pastiche, brass, mahogany and lots of mirrors, but it was the lighting that made it: hazy, reminiscent of gas mantles and fog-bound streets.

I didn't immediately recognize Chantal but my eyes were drawn, like everyone else's, to the lone woman sitting at the bar with the porcelain skin and the mane of dark brown ringlets. She nodded me to the stool beside her.

'You look so different!' I sounded gauche.

She smiled. Her teeth were small and very white against her copper lipstick. 'I wasn't at my best last time.'

'Clearly not.' She had on a short maroon velvet dress with a tightly fitted bodice. Her breasts were white and shadowed like mountains in a Japanese watercolour. I felt quite breathless.

'I haven't got long.' Her eyebrows were black and straight. There were two tiny lines between them now.

'No. Of course not. I wanted to ask you about the boy.'

'Wee Billie?'

'I thought you said his name was Kenny.'

'Oh, Rusty's baby. I thought you—'

'Who's Wee Billie?'

'Just a boy Rusty's friendly with. Hangs around the Dilly. Or did.'

'A boy? How old?'

'Looks about twelve. He's older than that, though. Been around for years. Rusty's sort of a mother to him.'

'Where would I find him?'

Chantal looked over her shoulder, then into her little beaded bag. 'Can you get us a drink? I should be started now.'

I bought the drinks. 'Chantal, where?'

'Oh, round and about. Come to think of it I ain't seen him this week. Everybody knows him. You'll find him. Just ask for Wee Billie.' She looked into the mirror over the bar. 'Look, I'm not being funny or nothing but can you go? Or sit somewhere else.'

I drained my half and said over-loudly, 'Nice seeing you, Chantal. I've got to go now,' and headed for the ladies' by the side door.

Chantal gave one last glance in the mirror and slid down off her stool. Three men got up at the same time. She stopped at the door and patted her hair in the reflection on the bottle-glass pane. One man followed her out.

wee billie

Wee Billie was a runner. That I discovered from a string of fruitless phone calls. Everybody knew of him, no one knew where he was. I got several 'If you do find him, let us know' replies. The police in particular were very keen to interview him.

'Not without an adult present, you don't,' I said.

He did have a surname, two in fact, but everybody, social workers, police, street kids and working girls, all called him Wee Billie. As far as I could gather, Rusty gave him the name when he first appeared, about two years ago.

That was discovery number two. Rusty was Scottish. No one had thought it worth mentioning. For me, it gave an ounce of extra substance to the wraith I was pursuing. She had an accent, 'not Glasgow, somewhere just outside'. A blurred ten-year-old photo, an echo of dialect, and the clothes she left behind. I wished I was a bloodhound so I could add her smell to the composite.

And now I was on the trail of a boy, almost as elusive, in the hope he'd lead me to her.

I had an appointment with someone who'd once been his key worker.

'What's he done? Everyone's suddenly very keen to find him. I'll tell you what I told the police.'

She gave me a lot of information about how he'd first come into care; his placement in a foster home, which seemed to be working out well when he suddenly ran away. He'd been running ever since.

'If he went back there, they'd tell us. He seems to have lost contact with them anyway. There's a note on file, from eighteen months ago, "Mr Wheeler died suddenly, of a stroke. Stephanie wants Billie to contact her urgently." Doesn't look like he ever got the message.'

'You mean you haven't seen him in eighteen months? But he's only fifteen now.'

'What are we supposed to do? You say he's not committed any offence. If we took him in it'd be for his own protection, but he'd only run away again. A secure unit wasn't felt to be appropriate.' She looked down at her hands helplessly. 'We're not getting very good publicity at the moment.'

'Were you ever?' I said, remembering my own frustrations in the job. 'You're damned if you leave them at home, damned if you take them away, damned if you lock them up and blamed if anything happens to them on the street.'

Something like relief flooded into her eyes: someone who understood. 'I worry about them all. I'll do anything in my power to help you find him. He's a lovely boy.'

'My problem is,' I said, 'I'm chasing a shadow. I don't have any picture of him. I know his history now, but I still haven't any idea where he'd take off to, what would be in his mind.'

She looked down at the buff file on her lap, fingered a paper-clip.

'What makes him different? Everybody seems to remember him. Why?' I looked straight into her eyes.

She dropped her gaze immediately. Her mouth was moving. She seemed to be debating something. She fiddled with the clip. 'I shouldn't be doing this.' She slid the black-and-white photo out from under it, handed it across to me.

'Here he is, Harry Houdini. We can't keep him under lock and key. Perhaps you'll do better.'

She had that same grey ironic smile I used to see in my own mirror. It had been my cue to quit while there was something left of me to get out. She'd probably left it too late. Still, she was a grown-up person. I wasn't going to tell her how to live her life. I returned a weak smile.

'Thanks. I'll take great care.'

I looked down at the picture. He had light-coloured eyes, grey or green I supposed, and very dark lashes, a pale elfin face, a puckish twist to his pretty mouth. Something squeezed my stomach: he was so small, so pretty. I didn't want to think what would happen to him on these streets. Something more than that, he looked familiar, that lop-sided smile. I thought I could hear sea in the distance. Whispering.

I shivered. 'Have the police got his description?' I wanted official reassurance.

'Of course, they know him well. He's a regular feature round these parts, but what can they do? There are too many. We were setting up a special unit for kids, young people, like Wee Billie who are uncontainable but shouldn't be locked up.' She shrugged. 'But, resources, reorganization, you know how it is.'

I knew how it was. I'd crept off to my little piece of private enterprise. I resented her making me feel guilty. The phone rang.

I pocketed the photo and jumped up. 'I've taken too much of your time already. I know how busy you are. Thank you so much.'

I was half-way out of the door before she could protest.

I made several copies of the picture in one of those instant photo labs and sent her the original back with profuse apologies for picking it up by mistake. It was the least I could do.

The air had taken on a new chill. It crept round my back. I felt under-dressed and exposed. I wondered if I should dig out my winter coat again.

I needed a drink. I didn't want to go back to the office. It suddenly seemed oppressive and pretentious. Had nowhere else to go, though. I found my feet carrying me that way.

I passed Evian working a regular patch. Street etiquette dictated I just nod and pass on, but she looped her arm through mine.

'Haydon, darling, long time no see,' she cried. 'Fancy a bevvy?'

She danced me through the back-streets on her clipping high heels to an afternoon-opening pub.

'You saved my life,' she hissed. 'I'm buying.'

'In that case, I'll have a double Irish with a glass of water separately.'

She had a gin with things floating in it and led me down to the basement. The bar wasn't open but the barman turned on the lights for us at a wiggle from Evian.

'You're hiding from somebody. Punter?'

She laughed. 'You won't believe it, Hallie. Same bloke twice in a day. I don't reckon to a third. Pushing my luck, I'd say.'

'I should think so. Do you mean he actually paid you money twice? Didn't he—'

'You have to reckon wi' em being daft. I just said I got moved on. I'd already paid out for the room, so if he wanted it he had to pay again.'

I shook my head. Then something occurred to me. 'Could Rusty have been clipping? Chantal insists that she wasn't on the game, but maybe she'd think it was different if she didn't actually deliver.'

Evian twiddled her olive, thoughtfully. 'Chantal doesn't want to believe Rusty was on the game. It doesn't mean anything either way. She did do private parties.'

'Do what?'

Evian speared a piece of greenery on her cocktail stick and shrugged. 'Danced. I don't know. Maybe like a stripper-gram. Not my type of party. Too rough.'

'Would she go off to one of these parties just like that? If someone stopped her on the street?'

'If the money was right.'

I showed her the picture of Wee Billie.

She nodded. 'Seen him around. Pretty lad.'

'That's what worries me. He looks so vulnerable. It's that lopsided smile. As soon as I saw this picture I was scared. He's so young.'

Evian picked up the glass of gin and swirled it under her nose. Spirit and vermouth slid gelatinously by. A dark green leaf sank half-way down the glass then surfaced.

'Evian, why do I think he's in danger?'

'Maybe you're psychic.' Her eyes grazed mine for a second. 'Maybe you know something and you're not telling.'

plague days

It was as if I bore the marks of some fatal contagious disease. People moved away from me, avoided me, fell silent as I approached. I carried with me, for the first time in my life, a ring of personal space upon which strangers intruded only fearfully.

I tried the boys begging at the underground stations.

'Do you know a lad called Wee Billie? Have you seen him lately?'

Silence, and after the first few encounters, vanishing. Why didn't the Metropolitan Police employ me to clear the streets of unwanted persons? I was doing a good job of it.

On the benches in Soho Square and the precincts of the shopping arcade only the drunks stayed for questioning.

'Gis a coupla bob for a cuppa tea, love.'

I tried bribery and it didn't work. I tried indignation at their demands for cans of Special Brew. I tried cunning. Nothing.

I sat on a bench and cried and all the company I got was pigeons and a mad woman.

I tried in the morning when dirty-faced boys were stirring in their sleeping bags in shop doorways, and the old Chinese women performed their slow exercises in the park. They ignored me like windmills.

I tried lunch-times when the messengers sprawled on

the grass in their tight Lycra and their big radio holsters. They shook their heads without interrupting their conversations.

Mid-afternoon was a slack time for the clubs and live shows. I thought I might chat to some of the girls. It didn't work out that way. I must have emanated unease. They disappeared behind curtains, clammed up when I addressed them directly and sent warnings along their secret telegraph so that I was expected and met by men in dark glasses and cheap imitations of designer suits.

I tried evenings as tired teenagers huddled round one cup of coffee at the late doughnut stall, and nights as they arranged their bits of cardboard.

Wee Billie had disappeared into a silence so deep it made my ears buzz.

I wanted to give up. I had plenty of other work to do. I had a conference paper to prepare, 'After-care of Violent Offenders', and I needed to chase the women's housing collective for a decision. This chase was a stupid indulgence. It was my time I was wasting, not some employer's. I was getting nowhere.

My failure snared me. It needled my professional pride. I was not one to take on a job and drop it for want of co-operation. That wasn't my style. People opened up to me. I was the listening ear. I wasn't easily put off. I hung in there until the time came. I wouldn't give up. It had always worked in the past. Somebody would talk.

Evian was a great help. I found her on her knees in my lobby with a nail-file. 'Lost something? Ask the great detective.'

'Not that raincoat, please, *chérie*. You don't want to look like Columbo.'

'It's a Burberry,' I objected.

'It's a jumble-sale Burberry. Don't think I don't know about your little Oxfam scam.'

I blushed.

The 'scam' had started some years ago at my mother's friend's house. She was throwing out some old clothes and my eye fell on a perfect unworn wool skirt. 'Don't,' I cried. 'Let me take them. I collect for Oxfam.' The little lie had grown monstrous. My whole flat now bulged with the leavings of the ladies in that corner of Surrey. Much of it did find its way to charity shops. But I discovered in myself a surprising covetousness. I had one whole wardrobe of evening dresses which I never wore outside. Coats, though, were rare. They were bought to be worn and not thrown out until they were worn out. Hence the shabby Burberry.

'Does it really look that bad?'

'*Je regrette* so. It's a *désastre*. No wonder nobody will speak to you.'

I didn't honestly believe that the homeless youth were that put off by my garb. When your luck's running low, though, you're more prone to superstition. So I agreed to a change of image.

Next evening I trotted off to the Lagoon (proprietor D. Grazeley) in a turquoise shot-silk evening gown. Shoes were a problem. I don't own any heels. The best I could manage was a pair of black kid slippers I'd bought on holiday in Italy.

I thought my luck would change with my clothes. I didn't reckon on it changing for the worse.

The place was tiny. Not much bigger than my spare room (the one with the wardrobes full of rejects). I reached it down a steep stairway that seemed to be wallpapered with black bin-liners. There was a minute bar at one end: a cocktail cabinet with a cheap sound system leaning on it.

There were tables along one wall, curtained off into separate booths but so close together you could hear everything. So much for blending in with the ambience.

I walked up to the bar. The girl looked scared.

'You the show?' she whispered.

I shook my head. 'No, I just want to talk.'

Her eyes swivelled frantically. 'Who you with?' She dipped down into the cabinet and pulled out a bottle of fizzy wine. It had a tinfoil wrapper and a plastic cap. My teeth were on edge just looking at it. 'Geezer in the corner waiting for company. Funny bugger. You're new, ain't yer? Take care.' She handed me two grey-smeared glasses.

The funny bugger in the corner was a good enough place to start I thought. I picked up the bottle and the glasses and rehearsed 'Come here often?' You never knew: he might have known Rusty.

Before I reached the corner I was intercepted by a gaunt, acne-scarred man in a shiny suit. Bad skin seemed to be a hazard of this kind of work. He flicked his head at me which I interpreted as meaning I should follow him. I held up the bottle and the glasses, and smiled coyly. His eyes spat at me. I followed.

He took me to an office the size of a shoebox. I put the bottle and the glasses down on the table. He looked me up and down in a cold, measuring manner. The bodice of my dress was too tight at the breast and too loose at the shoulder. My flesh bulged out sideways at the armpits. I fiddled with the neck to pull the slack to the back.

'What do you want here?'

'I just wanted to talk.' I wished I'd brought a wrap or a shawl. His eyes seemed to be weighing off my loose pounds on an invisible scale.

'You're frightening the girls.' He picked at my dress

material, ran it through his fingertips like rubbing in pastry. 'Nice.'

I brushed his hand off. He didn't even seem aware he was doing it. 'I'm not frightening them. They're scared of something. It's not me. I just want to know who knew Rusty.'

He shook his head. 'No, too much quality for this place.' His eyes couldn't keep away from my dress. I realized the fabric of his suit was a coarse imitation of it. 'Who cares about Rusty?'

'I do. I want to find her.'

'Cunt,' he said, lighting a small cigar. 'Plenty more where that came from. But.' He jabbed the cigar at me. 'When the girls get jumpy, the customers get nervous. Can't have that, can we?'

I backed away but there wasn't anywhere to go.

'Lovely dress. Delicate fabric, eh? Don't go upsetting Mr Grazeley. He's got friends.'

That answered one question. This, then, wasn't the boss. With as much dignity as I could muster, straightening my gaping neckline with one hand, I gave him my card. 'When Mr Grazeley sees fit to talk to me.'

He nodded a little sadly and escorted me off the premises. I was shaking when I hit the cold air of the street. He stood watching me for a long time, until I turned the corner.

burgled

I was furious with Evian. She'd got me into all this. In a small detached rational part of my mind I knew I was being unfair. That part of my mind was in suspension. The rest was dominated by waves of red nausea. Cramps. I could only shuffle along a few paces before being bent double again.

'You want to be a bloody woman,' I hissed. 'Try this.'

Evian wasn't there to hear me. What could she have done if she had been? Had a womb transplant? That wouldn't help me.

I was beyond caring about the curious looks I was getting. Someone offered me an arm. I shook it off, snarling. Finally, I found shelter in a doorway. I slid to the ground and rested my head against cool stone.

It was five o'clock, time for the evening rubbish collection. I shared the doorway with a shiny bulging black bag from the restaurant next door. It smelt sweet and bloody and familiar.

'Make it go away,' I groaned. 'Just make it go away.'

At the far end of the street I could hear the roar of the dust-cart, a grinding, wrenching shriek. I had to move before they reached me. I couldn't bear the way they would not look at me, carefully step round me. I'd done it myself, shrunk from contagion. Don't let me be mad.

I clawed my way upright. If I could get to my office,

39

there was a bottle of Black Bush in the safe, along with the ring. That ruby, I thought, spilling its bloody light, staining everyone who touched it. The perfect ruby, in hermetic philosophy, confers wisdom, beauty, joy in life. Like lithium, as they'd have you believe in hospital. Ha. Madness.

'Get up. Walk,' I commanded myself.

You're not mad, just premenstrual. Sometimes it was hard to tell the difference. I recited the symptoms of psychotic illness. Clinical paranoia: malign objects, disordered behaviour, terror, distrust of those closest . . . Who was I close to? I ate alone. I bought single tickets to the opera. Mania: euphoria, delusions, heightened perception, altered body image.

'Walk, damn you. Stand straight.'

I willed my spine straight. It cried out to curl and clutch at the ball of pain that burned in my lower back. I walked. Walked with a straight back and a wet face. In a while, my muscles submitted, loosed their hold on the pain. I had conquered it. I took slow, deep breaths. My head was full of triumphant white light. This must be how marathon runners feel as they force themselves through the wall.

The street door to my office was still open. I smiled at the brass plate.

'Haydon Aachen, where are you?' It seemed a good joke.

There was a scratch on the brass office door-lock. Careless. I had some polish in the tiny utilities cupboard. There I kept a small tool-kit, paint, plugs and fuses. Most of them were still in their shrink-wrapped packets. I bent to open the cupboard.

What was it that distinguished suspicion from paranoia? The level of fear? Faulty reasoning?

Someone had been in my office. I didn't know how I knew. Not from the scratch on the door-lock alone, though that was a clue. Something in the air? I sniffed hard. Dust.

A faint solvent smell from correcting fluid, whiteboard cleaner, felt tips. Warm oil, and was it ozone? A smell that was like a hum. I went round touching the word-processor, photocopier, radiator, extractor. Nothing was warm. Nothing felt recently used. I sniffed the handset of the telephone. My palms were slippery.

'Is this the behaviour of a rational person?' I asked.

The office did not reply.

Logic. Rationality. If the office had been broken into, what was missing?

The safe, I was prepared to swear, had not been opened. The ring was there in its blue bag. The ruby winked sarcastically, untouched. My uncompleted VAT returns, which I'd placed there more for effect than importance, were exactly as I'd left them.

I took out the bottle of Black Bush and poured myself a large one. I had a mini-fridge for milk, but when I looked the ice-cube tray was empty.

'Yes, Officer, the thieves made off with several ice cubes.' No, it wouldn't do. I couldn't go to the police. Hysterical woman. I had to sit down. I felt sick.

No equipment had been stolen. My files, so far as I could see, were all in order. I emptied my waste bin on to the table. Every piece of paper but one I recognized. It was crumpled, blank apart from a blue pen stroke, top left. A single vertical line: 'I' or '1'.

The start of a note: 'I called in but . . . ?' Number one of a list? Or just an accidental pen line that rendered the sheet unusable for a top copy. It was high-quality recycled paper, watermarked. I could see the box it had come from open on the shelf. Next to it the lid held scrap for notes. See, I didn't waste paper. I didn't throw away a whole sheet for one mark.

To me that sheet was proof enough. I knew it wouldn't

stand up in court. Who, and why? Evian was prime suspect. That new lock was a challenge to her. She might have broken in just to show she could. Maybe she started writing me a note and then thought better of it.

I couldn't smell her perfume, and there were no ends in the ashtray.

If not Evian, who? Someone who knew I'd be out of the way, so they could search my office. What for? Grazeley, if he thought I was getting too close, would want to know what I knew. I giggled. The whiskey was making me skittish. If only you knew, Mr Grazeley, how little I know. So Grazeley, or his men, had searched and found nothing, for there was nothing to find.

What would they do next? It was darker now and the street ill-lit. My defences against the outside seemed suddenly flimsy. I turned on the desk lamp. The strewn paper leapt at me, familiar yet charged with menace. Pull yourself together. How can you be scared of a piece of paper?

I dropped each piece in the basket individually: circulars, special offers and half-written letters. It wasn't true that I never wasted paper. Don't give in to paranoia. You'll end up back in hospital. The edifice of suspicion was fragile. The conspiracy could be blown away as lightly as a ball of crumpled paper.

'Stop it, H. Get out. To the opera, to see *Tosca*.'

I drained the whiskey. It had relaxed the knot of tension. A warm fire seeped up my spine. A little fear is a good thing, self-protective. I should go armed. There were no guns or knives to be had. The best I could find in the little utilities cupboard was a small spray can of gold paint. I slipped it in my bag.

I was half-way down the street when the thought hit me: Wee Billie's photo was missing.

the fat lady sings

The desk sergeant eyed the wilting turquoise silk and, though he kept his expression carefully neutral, scepticism seeped from every pore.

In the glass door pane I'd seen a sooty smear on my forehead. How does soot manage to accumulate in a brand new office cupboard? I supposed he'd smelt the whiskey on my breath too.

He looked bored. He did most of his communicating with his eyebrow. He registered my presence, pointed out that there was someone before me and asked me to form an orderly queue, all with tiny movements of that one muscle. Because I am naturally obedient and needed space to recover my thoughts, I nodded humbly and took a plastic seat.

The woman ahead of me was becoming hysterical. She kept gulping air like a drowning fish. 'But he's only a lad,' she wailed. Gulp. 'What am I supposed to do?'

That was the most coherent she could manage. I thought she would have benefited from my communication-skills workshop. What a mean little thought. To be fair to myself, I take refuge in smugness when I'm frightened. I kept getting little shoots of panic, like injections, that made me sit straight in my seat and hope I wasn't twitching.

There is something horribly disturbing about a burglary where nothing is taken. Nothing except a photograph. It's like a big arrow descending from the sky, pointing. This is the one. This is where the danger is.

Everything about Billie exuded vulnerability. He was small for his age, big-eyed, pretty. He was behind educationally. No one could tell if he had learning difficulties or if he'd just missed too much school. Something in that lopsided smile spelt tragedy about to happen. Then there was his uncanny resemblance to the other boy, the one who died. I found myself shaking. I didn't want to think about all that.

I concentrated on reading the posters. One warned against pickpockets and another promoted Neighbourhood Watch. There were cigarette burns in the grey vinyl, even though the 'No Smoking' notice was clear.

Finally, the sobbing woman subsided into a chair. I approached the desk.

'I want to report a burglary,' I said in a clear, important, good-citizen voice, trying by my confident tone to distance myself from her.

Both eyebrows went up. He reached for a form. 'I'll just take your name and someone will be down to see you.' He picked up a phone and spoke some numbers into it.

I resumed my seat.

A man came in to argue about a parking fine. He was given a phone number and asked to call back in office hours.

Two women came in talking, and the desk sergeant released an electronic door-lock to let them through to the private offices.

A surly young man came in to show his insurance documents.

A woman in a green wool suit came in and sat down.

A teenage boy was brought out, shuffling and looking down at his curling trainers. He was reunited with his weeping mother. She stood up straight, pulled at his jacket and brushed back his hair as if she wanted to hit him. They went out silently.

A young officer with short sandy hair and acne replaced the sergeant at the desk. He started drawing hexagons on the back of a Crime Stoppers leaflet.

The green-suited woman went up to the desk and asked for a detective by name.

'He'll be down in a minute, madam.'

I asked if anyone was coming to deal with my case.

'Sorry, love, Burglary Squad are all nine-to-fivers. Someone will come to take your statement soon.'

'I'm not your love,' I said, between gritted teeth but not loudly.

I sat down. I made eye contact with the other woman, trying, by grimace, to suggest the solidarity of the waiting public. Her eyes cut me dead. I felt sick. For an instant there had been a flicker of recognition.

'Doctor Penrose.' Someone came to greet her from the locked offices and she followed him through.

Doctor Alice Penrose, forensic psychiatrist. I had a brief paranoid vision of her sharing her clinical knowledge of me with the detective. 'You have an ex-patient of mine in your waiting room. Interesting case, borderline, we couldn't agree on a diagnosis. My colleague went for manic depressive. Not actively psychotic, but self-dramatizing, not to be trusted. Unreliable as a witness.'

I took a deep breath. Talk about self-fulfilling prophecies. Relax. Medical ethics prevent the sharing of such secrets. Besides, I wasn't really her patient. I wasn't important enough to have my own consultant. I just saw her at the hospital. She probably didn't recognize me from there anyway. I'd met her more recently in her role as forensic psychiatrist at a conference called 'Illness and Punishment – dealing with the mentally disordered offender'. If she knew me at all it was from there, not from years before. I had to keep a lid on these fantasies or I would end up an unreliable witness.

When I'd finally given up hope and my legs were welded to the plastic chair seat, someone came to take my statement. He didn't look much more than a boy, in a creased leather jacket. He let me past the locked door to a little room. The first thing he did, as he glanced down at the sheet, was yawn.

'DC Rice. Burglary, right?'

I nodded.

'Arkin. Got a first name?'

I spelt out my name and corrected the pronunciation. He took my home and office address, status, profession. He muttered to himself as he took down the details. I imagined him saying, 'Blimey, got a right one here.'

'So, you got a full list of what's missing?'

I took a deep breath. 'Well, the thing is . . .'

He looked spitefully at the turquoise dress where it gaped at the armhole. 'Don't tell me, you were looking after a whole bunch of jewellery you forgot to tell your insurance company about.'

'No, quite the opposite. I did have a ruby ring in the safe but that wasn't touched. In fact, there's nothing of value missing.'

'You think they'll come back for another go, with the proper tools next time?' He had been looking tired but now he perked up.

'No. Well, I don't think so. I don't know. The only thing I can find missing is a photo. Of a boy. I'm worried something may happen to him.'

'Your child, is he?'

'No. I haven't actually met him. I'm looking for him. I think he may be in danger.'

He had put down his pen and was gazing up at the ceiling. Praying to a god he didn't believe in.

'I know this might sound strange,' I said. 'I don't normally dress like this. I'm going to the opera.'

'Covent Garden?' He wasn't interested. He hadn't picked up his pen.

'Yes, *Tosca*.'

'Wish I had your sort of money. So. You want to report a burglary where nothing is stolen and a missing child you've never met?'

'If you put it like that. I believe it's connected to another missing person. I reported her missing, so it should be under either her name, Stirling, or mine.'

He looked at me for several long seconds. He seemed like a man sorely tried. But what could I do?

Finally, he went over to the wall phone and buzzed an extension. 'Charlie? Oh, is he? Lucky bleeder. Yeah, can you look up a miss. pers. for us? Name of Stirling, reported by a H. Aching. Yeah, got her here now. No, Aachen. A-a-c-h-e-n. Thanks.'

He put the phone down and sat in front of me. 'No record of any missing-person report attached to either of those names. Are you sure you reported it? Didn't just think of doing so and then change your mind?'

'I don't change my mind,' I snapped. As soon as I said it, I thought it was the wrong thing to say. It made me sound rigid, fanatical. 'Look, please could you check again.'

I got out my diary. 'It was last Tuesday. I don't know who took the report and they didn't give me a reference number. Please double check.'

He tapped his pen against his teeth. 'OK. I'll go down there. Charlie who's usually on records has gone home. Maybe they didn't look properly. I'll go myself.' He gave me a hard look as if to say, 'You'd better not be giving me the run-around.'

He locked the door behind him. I had a second's panic when I thought he was going to consult with Dr Penrose. 'I've got a mad woman in my interview room. Dressed like the Queen of Sheba, with a big soot mark on her face, talking about phantom burglaries and missing persons. Think she's dangerous?'

I tried to calm myself down. It doesn't work like that. She wouldn't divulge that sort of information. Anyway, he's gone to check records. I am behaving like a responsible citizen. They're always going on about reporting anything suspicious.

There was nothing to read on the walls. I was tempted to open the file and see what he had written about me. I was afraid of leaving prints. I sat on my hands and waited.

Rice came back in. He didn't look pleased. 'Miss Arkin, I have gone through the files myself. There is no missing-person report under that name, or for that date. I don't know whether you are confused or this is some deliberate game, but I have to warn you there are penalties for wasting police time. Now shall we leave the missing person and return to the so-called burglary?'

The sensible thing would be to agree that I must have made a mistake. Something in me revolted. I'd felt a physical shock when he denied a report had been made. I knew I had made it. I hadn't imagined it. I was on the verge of tears. 'Look, it must be your mistake. I did make that report.'

'The only mistake is me sitting here and listening to you

48

for half an hour. Look, just give me the details of the burglary, then we can all go home. Items missing: one photo. Framed?'

'No, it was just a copy from the instant photo place. Five by seven. I did make that report. Someone must have stolen it.'

He blew out loudly through his teeth. 'A lot of bits of paper get stolen while you're around, Miss Aching. This is a police station. We're a little security-conscious here. Call us old-fashioned, but we like to keep things under lock and key. Now how do you suppose a thief would break into a police station to steal one of our files? The file, surprise surprise, that relates to your alleged missing person.'

'You can't speak to me like that. What about the Citizen's Charter? I want to make a complaint. I demand to speak to your superior officer. I have rights.' This would have been a more impressive performance had it not been accompanied by a rising sob. However, it worked. He must have been on a course.

He put his pen down and lifted the phone. 'Front desk? Where's Sarge? Well, give him a bell. Public Complaints Procedure. Yeah, sure. Cup of tea would be nice.' He put the phone down and addressed me. 'Inspector Tennyson is in charge of complaints this week. He or his sergeant will be down to see you shortly. I'm going off duty.'

A grey head poked round the door. 'Rice, is this the complainant? I've just got to have a quick word with Lance before he goes off.'

There was another man behind him, taller and wider with a mass of black curly hair. 'No, you sort this, guv. I can hang on for a few minutes.'

The grey-haired man, who introduced himself as DI Tennyson, took Rice's seat. Rice stood up with his head down. The other man stood by the door trying to blend in with the paintwork, which wasn't easy for a man of his size.

'Now, Ms Aachen,' he said, reading off my form. 'Ah! Burglary. Very upsetting. We do have a formal complaints procedure, which I will outline for you. But before we do that, let's see if we can work this one out between ourselves. Now, I know a crime of this nature can be terribly distressing and things can get a little heated if you feel you're not being listened to. Have you been given the Victim Support number?' He handed me across a leaflet. 'So what's been happening here?'

He was very soothing. I was beginning to think I'd overreacted. It was only sarcasm, after all.

'Well, Inspector, there does seem to be a problem about being believed here. I made a missing-person report the other day. I definitely did, I didn't imagine it. Now there's no record of it. When I suggested to the constable that the file may have been mislaid, he responded with undisguised sarcasm.'

'Oh dear,' said Tennyson.

Rice looked suitably contrite. It was obviously an act they'd worked out between them. Still, I'd have my pound of flesh. 'I don't really want to make a formal complaint. An apology would suffice.'

'Well?' said Tennyson.

Rice was silent.

'I'm afraid I can't guarantee that our records are a hundred per cent,' said Tennyson. 'Things do get misfiled. What was the name?'

'Stirling. I made the report last Tuesday.'

The man at the door coughed. 'A word, Inspector.'

Tennyson looked up, surprised. 'Say it, Lance.'

'Excuse me, miss. I think I may be able to clear up this

difficulty.' He looked genuinely embarrassed; his handsome face was blushing. 'I pulled that missing-person report. The woman was known to me. Goes under the name of Rusty S.'

I nodded. 'That's right.'

'It never got to the computer. I saw the alleged missing person after she was supposed to be missing. At Euston Station, coming out of the ticket office. Looked to me like she was going home. She's Scottish, the overnight train was due out. Sorry.'

'Was there anyone with her?'

'Not that I saw, but they might have been waiting while she bought the tickets. I'm terribly sorry if you've been inconvenienced, Miss . . .'

'Aachen,' Tennyson put in. 'Well, that seems to be that. Use the right form next time, Lance. And you, Rice, might like to apologize to Ms Aachen for your tone.'

anima mea

I was exhilarated by *Tosca*. I had two whiskeys and an ice cream in each interval. Apple-crumble and toffee-almond flavour. Hot and cold and music that swirled rich and dark round my spine. It lifted the ache and the fear high, clean away.

I skipped in the street. On the station platform, I leaned close to search for little mice between the lines. Until I heard the rails singing. The siren song. Tosca's cloak had billowed out as she went over. The wings of the aria filled my head with rushing sound. You didn't think you'd escape so easily. I am not mad. Knuckled panic gripped my throat. I floundered through the blanket of people closing on the oncoming train. Escape.

I'd known two other people throw themselves under trains. Both diagnosed manic depressive. I had to get out. The past lurked here, the thing I could neither remember nor forget. Stephenson never knew what he'd started with the steam engine.

I needed to eat. I was slipping into an old pattern, fasting and fainting. I'd be hallucinating next.

Perhaps I should sleep at the office on the little camp bed. I drifted in that direction, then changed my mind. The streets were full of light and hurrying people. It was raining. I laughed and put on my dark glasses. Then headed for a pizza at Great Windmill Street, but it was closing. There was a late doughnut and croissant place just by Piccadilly Circus. It had a queue already. I pressed up close to the steamy glass to peer at the greasy pastries. Someone jogged my elbow. I turned. It was the man from the Blue Lagoon. Fetish fingers. He didn't see me in my glasses. I thought of the missing photo and my burglarized office.

I fled down the nearest tube entrance. Little knots of youths held themselves apart from the flow of late passengers pressing for the last trains. I approached one group. They dispersed. I heard, passed between them like a last smoke, the whisper 'Law'.

I was angry. All I'd done for these people. I'd put myself at risk. I'd gone places that made my skin crawl. I'd been patronized and insulted by the police. How dare they? I started chasing after them. It was useless. They were like ghosts. I kicked the marble tiles of the subway wall. It was dark and I was alone.

Then I remembered the spray can. All of my life I have respected the law. I abhor vandalism. I pay my taxes. I don't drop litter. I epitomize respectable citizenry. All my bloody life. And where had it got me?

'I hate the law', I sprayed. 'Pigs', 'Filth', and then words I wasn't even aware were in my vocabulary.

The spray spluttered. Greeny-gold blobs dribbled down my fingers. I threw down the can with a curse. I heard a small giggle, but the creature scuttled away before I could see it.

I was pretty sure I'd missed my last tube. Anyway, the wind in the tunnel scared me. I couldn't trust myself in this state. I was tired. I'd have to sleep at the office.

The rain had stopped. The streets were dark and shiny. Occasional too-loud laughs from late revellers broke the quiet hum. It was never entirely silent.

53

Rain dripped on me from an awning. I shivered and took off the ridiculous glasses. What was I thinking of? I wondered at the wisdom of sleeping in an office that had already been broken into once today. If a taxi came by, I decided I'd flag it down.

Someone mumbled at me from a doorway. I jumped, then felt guilty. At least I had a bed for the night. It must be safer than sleeping on the street.

I talked to myself and all the time at the edge of my awareness something was gathering. I first registered it as heat on my skin, and a pain under my ears as they tensed listening. A sound within a sound, a shadow out of the corner of my eye; someone, something – no, definitely a person, was following me. Two legs because it kept in time with my steps.

I slowed and speeded up and it did the same. But there was something animal about it, feral: the way it could see in the dark and know before I did that I was going to turn. My clothes felt wetter inside than out. My body smell seemed to fill the street. How could it fail to track me?

The last corner. I could run from here. I wasn't exactly scared, more spooked. The uncanny. I was dripping hot and slick with dread. It was following my scent as if the damp rising from me were a ribbon connecting us. I had an impression of doggedness.

The pun gave it away. Dogged. Dog. Animal. Anima. I laughed out loud in the street and swung round to face it. There was nothing. Of course. This bloodhound that haunted my steps came from within: my unconscious. One does not come face to face with that very often.

I let myself in at the downstairs door. I was careful to double-lock it. Seeing a ghost in the street does not negate the real dangers that come from the world of men. My office door I locked and wedged with a chair and the photocopier. I knew the lock on its own wasn't sufficient.

My heart-rate was slowing but I still felt a pain like a big boulder in my chest. The windows across the alley were blank. Something dark gleamed from the corner.

I pulled down my own shade to be sure. I imagined a small, hunched figure, not quite human, squatting in the wet light reflected off the cobblestones, keeping its vigil; its bright animal eyes never sleeping. It was a curiously comforting idea.

I took out the fold-up bed. It was smaller and meaner than I remembered it. The metal frame shrieked as I opened it out. The bare springs squealed. I had a tartan picnic blanket but no pillow. I undressed to my underwear and spread my coat over the blanket. It was damp and steamed like an animal let in from the cold.

The back pain was returning. I couldn't curl up in the bed: it was too narrow. I lay stiff and straight as a stick and tried to find my willpower. I needed a hot-water bottle or a massage. Cold crept in round the edges of the blanket. Relax, I told myself. Pain was radiating like pulled strings along my thighs. I lay for a long time whispering, 'Make it go away.' Mind over matter wasn't working.

At the clinic they said orgasm was the best relief for pelvic congestion.

'Oh yes,' I said. 'Have you got any more helpful suggestions?'

I daren't use that route. Whenever I let myself go, just before the climax, I was haunted by that face. Carole playing with her wedding ring, her green eyes cruel and inviting. Carole rubbing my hand: 'I'll stay with you, but I really think you need to see a doctor.' Carole, whom I trusted, whom I valued above my sanity. When the doctor came he asked me the name of the Prime Minister.

Any physical agony was preferable to those memories. Keep with the abstract.

I rubbed my stomach and the tops of my thighs. Warmth was beginning to soften the edges of pain. I concentrated on my inner breathing. Behind my closed eyes, I saw my womb red and congested with blood. Relax. Breathe.

I clenched my fists and dug my knuckles into the bottom of my belly. Her green, lying eyes danced before me. I wished my body could be sleek and mechanical, needing only an oil and a polish to function smoothly. I kneaded the skin at the top of my legs, concentrating on quadratic equations.

It was harder to focus on my breathing. When the red images danced on my retina, I slowed my hands and started counting. Prime numbers, prime suspect. Ruby, Rusty. Eleven, thirteen, seventeen. I couldn't remember what came next.

The spring squeaked. Carole, no. Nineteen, twenty-one. Not twenty-one. I pressed my legs into the canvas bed base. I could feel my breath massing in my chest like before lightning.

Sweat gathered in the hollow of my back. I pushed it down. Are you sure you didn't imagine this? You need to see a doctor. Car— No. Twenty-three. My breath was rasping in my throat like fire. The bed leg rattled. The pain pulled itself into a shrinking ball, imploding. Gravity left my body.

I floated, weightless, over to the window and looked out. My guardian angel, crouched like a stone in the alley, kept watch.

bernie

Sunlight came in bright and painful through the blinds. It must be very late or very hot. I scanned the room with one eye. One side of my face and the arm I lay on were numb. I had an excruciating pain over the other eye. I poked round inside my cheek with my tongue. It felt like thick rubber. My teeth had something woolly knitted on to them.

Got to get rid of the bloody light. A lump of nausea pushed at my throat. I was having some horrible dream. Gremlins and spray paint. I rubbed my eye. My fingers glinted at me, green and metallic. Go back to sleep, you've turned into a robot. I tried to think peaceful dreams of long, empty beaches, but metal mermaids threw clods of obscenities at me. Wake up, it's not worth it.

I rolled myself off the bed. The bump jarred my limbs into life. I crawled over to the kettle. My fingers really were green. I'd deal with that in a minute. I put my raincoat on over my underwear and went to fill the kettle in the small kitchen/bathroom I shared with the others in the building. I prayed none of them would be in.

A solicitor from downstairs was coming out of the men's toilet. I ducked into the ladies'. He'd looked away. He hadn't finished doing himself up. I put the kettle down, and stood listening against the toilet door, until his footsteps were lost in the carpet at the bottom of the stairs.

There was a small handbasin in the ladies'. It was awkward

getting the kettle under the tap but I didn't want to risk the sink in the kitchen until I looked more human. The green wouldn't come off my hands. There was a lot more on the right than the left.

A pink-eyed harridan signalled despair at me from the mirror. Well, detective, what do you make of that? I must have been very drunk. It wasn't just a dream about spraying obscenities. I threw water at the face but it didn't get any prettier.

Plan. Number one, tea. I drew a '1' with my finger on the mirror. I looked at myself curiously. The sheet of paper. The start of the paranoia. If the someone who had broken into my office had been so far gone with drink or drugs, and had started making a list . . . Stop it, H. Tea first.

The milk was on the turn. I swilled the tea round in the mug and it separated out into cream-coloured flakes. It had a tang that was not wholly unpleasant. I left half a cup. Cappuccino and croissants, that's what I needed.

I had a quick shower in the little room off the kitchen. The water was warm but the jet holes were blocked and it came out in big soft dollops instead of fine bracing needles. I had a box of paper panties in my drawer but otherwise had to dress in yesterday's clothes. To my mental list I added a spare set of clothes along with the pillow.

The French patisserie was too crowded. There was another a few streets away. It was odd to think these were the same streets. Soho keeps to a different clock from the rest of the world. Things open at night; the streets are swept; the bins emptied. Morning finds it tired and hung-over, sour with last night's debris.

Someone was walking behind me. 'All right?'

I wheeled round. 'No, I'm not all right. I have intense premenstrual cramps, dehydration, nausea. Shall I go on?'

It stepped back, then grinned a big monkey grin. 'Buy us a hamburger?'

'Why?'

'You're looking for someone.'

It wasn't immediately obvious what sex the monkey was. Closer inspection revealed a small black and mauve badge on the dusty bomber jacket which proclaimed, 'So what I'm a dyke?' The syntax irritated me: it might be all right in Brooklyn, but not here. Still, it was as effective a gender-signal as any pink ribbon.

'So, what do you know?'

'He's my friend, Wee Billie. I'm his sort of god-mother.'

I thought: This boy has a surfeit of mothers. I said, 'I'm going for a coffee and a cake. Want to come?'

She padded along beside me, as if she'd always been there. And maybe she had. We found half a table at the Italian coffee house. When I ordered a cappuccino and *pain au chocolat* she nodded for the same. Sitting next to each other, her head barely cleared my shoulder.

'So what's your name? I'm Haydon. You can give me a made-up name, White Lightning, Mountain Spring, if you like.'

She looked sideways at me. 'Bernie. Short for Bernadette, but I don't like it, makes me think of Lourdes.'

She pronounced it like the cricket ground. I was puzzled for a moment. 'Ah, Saint Bernadette. And how do you know Wee Billie?'

'Like I said, I looked after him. He was really small when he first came to London. He needed someone to look out for him.'

How touching. 'And how long ago was that?' I asked.

She counted off on her fingers. 'Three, four years ago.

I'm eighteen now, that's how I can talk to you. So he must have been about eleven then.'

The cuff of her jacket pulled back and I saw a railway track of fine scars crossing her wrist. Trouble.

'That's terribly young.'

'That was the first time. Then he went back to Southport. Came back here about two years ago for good.'

'So where is he now?'

'Haven't seen him for weeks. Never been gone this long before, except when he went home that time.'

'Home? Where's that?'

'I told you. Southport. Southsea. Something like that. It was a seaside place. He used to tell me about it.' When she smiled her little ugly face turned cute, like a certain sort of small dog, a Pekinese or chihuahua.

'If it was so idyllic why did he come back to sleep on the streets of Soho?'

She screwed up her face, as if she didn't understand the question. She did, though. 'It was the dad. He didn't get on with him. It was a foster family. He liked the mum but not the dad. He don't really like men. Like me.' She pointed proudly to her badge.

'I saw it,' I said.

The waitress who brought us our cappuccino saw the badge too. She gave me a filthy look.

'She thinks I'm a child molester,' I told Bernie.

Bernie grinned and wriggled closer to me.

I thought of the fine wrist-slash scars and pushed her away. 'Drink your coffee. You can spoon the top off. That's the best bit.'

She swirled her spoon round the top of the white foam, mixing it in with the chocolate flakes. She licked it slowly. 'Do you like girls?'

60

'That's not a proper question. The woman I'm looking for disappeared the Friday before last. Was Billie around then?'

Bernie bit on the spoon. 'Yes,' she said, after a moment.

'Yes definitely or yes maybe?'

'Definitely. She was going to buy him a doughnut.'

'Who was?'

'The woman you're looking for.'

The chocolate croissants came. I felt I'd missed something somewhere. 'Did you see him after that?'

She didn't answer immediately. Her mouth was full of golden pastry and chocolate. There were flakes of it on her upper lip. She ate like an animal.

'I didn't see him,' she said. 'Someone says they did. Early in the morning and he was scared, talking about hiding out. Something about a car. I don't know whether to believe them. Sometimes people tell you stories just to make themselves sound interesting.'

'Yes, they do,' I said. I thought: Southport trains leave from Euston. They could have gone together. I wasn't sure what to make of Bernie. 'Why are you telling me all this now? Nobody else has been willing to talk about Billie.'

'They saw you going into the cop shop, talking to that man. They didn't know where you were coming from.'

'And you do?'

She giggled. 'I know you're not the law now. I got this feeling you won't hurt Billie.'

She slipped an arm through mine as I got up to pay the bill. I removed it. 'I wouldn't hurt anyone deliberately. But that's not always good enough.'

I didn't like it when she followed me back to the office. I stopped to buy a paper, but she waited with me.

'Do you often sleep in your office?' she asked.

I didn't ask how she knew. 'No.'

'Can I?'

'What?'

'Can I sleep in your office, if you're not using it?'

'No.'

I had to give her credit: she didn't point out that her alternative was sleeping on the streets, that she could be raped or murdered and nobody would know or care. She just walked along beside me in silence.

At the street door, she said, 'I could be a sort of guard dog.'

I held up the newspaper as a shield. 'It says here they've found the torso of a woman in a wood in Surrey.'

She looked at me.

I said, 'Torso means the body without the arms and legs and head.'

dorking

Surrey is a big place I kept telling myself. My mother lived in Surrey: it didn't make her a murderer. I had no reason to believe the body was Rusty's. Just a shiver at the base of my spine. Don't go sloppy about intuition, H. You find connections because you look for them.

My mother had rung yesterday with the Deerharts' home address. It was a village just outside Dorking. I asked her what it was like.

'Lovely. Surprisingly wooded. It's chalk escarpment—'

'Mother, I don't want a geology lesson. What are the houses like?'

'All sorts, really. All sorts of ages. They have some original Tudor, and even earlier. I think there was some sort of monastery, with vineyards and things. Time of the Black Prince. Goodness, my memory's going. I used to be able to reel all this stuff off. Why are you asking, dear? You're not thinking of . . . ?'

'You don't give up, do you, Mother? No, I'm not thinking of. He's married already. This is just a work matter.'

She gave a sceptical hum down the phone. 'Work. Hmm. What is this "Aachen" business? I hope it's not some feminist nonsense. Your grandmother would turn in her grave to have the name used so.'

'No, it's not feminist, it's just a business decision.'

'Oh, and "Haydon"?'

'Haydon's Road. It's a railway station on the Wimbledon line.'

The silence at the other end of the phone was very loud. Finally, 'But it was so long ago. Darling, you can't—'

'No, Mother. Not that.' I put the phone down.

I immediately picked it up again. I stared at it. There was a whistling like wind in an exposed place. The cable wormed towards me like a malign intestine.

Put the phone down. Take a deep breath. Stop the craziness. It is all right to have hunches. Normal people act on hunches. A body is found in Surrey. John Deerhart lives in Surrey. A tenuous connection, but real. Phone him. Forget the other stuff.

For the rest of the afternoon I applied myself diligently to the resources section of the training pack I was putting together. I hadn't made up my mind what sort of cross-referencing system to use yet: everything overlapped with everything else. I shuffled loose papers across my desk, waiting for inspiration. A sheet caught my eye from a resettlement project:

CRIME? Nobody's found the cure, but we're working on prevention.

I felt a ping in my brain as a bulb lit up. Crime prevention. Why hadn't I thought of it before? They were professionally obliged to pander to paranoia. I could show them the scratch on my lock and they'd congratulate me on my observation. The cold, rational part of my brain asked: Why are you so desperate for vindication? Losing your nerve, H.?

The Crime Prevention Officer wasn't available, but they logged my request. I told them my address and office hours.

I had a visit from Evian. 'Do you know there's been a black car parked on the corner three times this week?'

'Must be a lucky black car, not to have got clamped. Still the Crime Prevention Officer will sort it out. He's due any minute.'

'The what? Must be off, urgent business.'

'Bye. Do tell me if you see anything else suspicious.' I wondered if my little guard dog was still hanging around outside.

He arrived just as I was closing up. Inspector Tennyson. I'd met him before.

'We have a request for someone to come out and check your security. Is that right, miss?'

'Yes, I called this afternoon. Have I seen you before? Have you been in Crime Prevention long?'

'You could say that, miss. Now, was there any special reason for calling us, or just general concern?'

'I think the door-lock's been tampered with. There's a scratch on it I didn't make, and nobody else has legitimate access to this room.'

He bent to examine the lock. 'Very observant, miss: it's not a big scratch. Very succinctly put case. I wish all our reports were so clear.'

The light winked off his short grey hair. 'You were at the police station.'

'Very likely, miss, being a police officer and all.'

'They were very rude and unhelpful. I could have put in a complaint.'

'But you didn't, miss.'

'It's not too late, Officer. Why have you come round here impersonating a Crime Prevention Officer?'

'Impersonating, that's a little strong. I'm an officer of the Metropolitan Police, my brief is crime prevention and apprehending felons. There's no misrepresentation involved.'

'What are you doing here?'

'Exactly what I said I was doing when I introduced myself. I have come to check your doors, windows, locks, safes, whatever security measures, and advise you where in my opinion they need strengthening. I came to check if you were all right. What's your business, Miss Aachen?'

'What?'

'What do you do? What's your work? Do you handle large amounts of money or valuables, sensitive documents? Is there anything that makes you particularly vulnerable? Do you work alone? Late? Nights?'

'What business is it of yours?' I was nearly screaming.

He took a deep breath and sat himself down. 'Shall we start again, Miss Aachen? I see you have a kettle. Do you think we could have a cup of tea and talk about it?'

'There's no milk.' I could feel the anger hissing out of me like a slow puncture.

'There's a supermarket across the way. I'll fetch you a carton of milk, and you put the kettle on and have a think about my questions.'

It was difficult to hold on to my anger. No police officer had ever bought me a carton of milk. They were quick enough to order the kettle on. They even occasionally offered one tea, lukewarm grey slops. My nearly sub-merged rational self said one carton of milk did not a confessor make. But I was tired. I didn't have the energy to go mad.

We sipped our tea.

'Lovely cup. You should see the rubbish they serve down at the station. You'd go a long way to find worse. Now, Miss Aachen, let me explain my questions. You see, we need to know what we're guarding against. Is it the opportunist thief, or could you be targeted?'

I shivered.

'I see you're feeling vulnerable. You've come to the right place. You'd be amazed the number of people who try to deal with these things themselves, young ladies with big knives in their handbags.' He shook his head. 'You've done the right thing, Miss Aachen.'

He hummed around poking my windows and my equipment. 'I see you've got a word-processor, Miss Aachen. You know, I've noticed a curious thing. Now that we're all much more used to computers we start giving them female names. MAVIS. DORA. I should think you'd have something to say on that.'

I didn't. But his affability wore me down. I gave him details of my work, my usual habits, I even confided about the suspected break-in.

'Nothing taken?'

Just in time I stopped myself mentioning the photo of Billie. I shook my head with bitten lips.

'You'll never know for sure.'

He gave me several leaflets on personal safety, recommended window-locks, wired glass and new deadlocks for the office door.

'My, er, friend said that lock wasn't as solid as it looked,' I said.

'What's he? A burglar?' he joked.

I didn't laugh. 'There's one other thing. I put in a missing-person report.'

'Oh, yes.'

'Well, you know there's a body been found in Surrey. Any chance of . . . ?' I didn't know how to ask.

'Not really my department. I'll put the word round,

though. They're a good bunch of lads. Anyone knows anything they'll tell me. Redhead, isn't it? That'll speed up identification. You all right?'

I'd dropped my cup and was staring at him. 'There's nothing in the papers about it being a redhead.'

'Sorry, miss. I meant your missing person. My sergeant was on duty the night she disappeared. He keeps an eye on the clubs. I don't know about the body. Should be easy enough to check, though, with the local force. I'll make you another cup.'

I dabbed at the spilt tea with tissues. It had been nearly empty anyway. How did he know about Rusty?

He must have sensed the question. He handed me the tea and said, 'Research always helps. When we get one of these requests for a visit, we like to check up whether we've got anything else on that address on file. You know, reported break-ins, attacks, muggings. Saves us from treading on too many toes. Marvellous what you can call up on a computer.'

'So you'll have all my details, every contact I've had with the police?' I looked him straight in the eye.

He smiled. It was stupid trying to psych out an old policeman. 'I am truly sorry about that, Miss Aachen. It was my sergeant sorted you out. One of the reasons I wanted to come over myself and see if you were all right.'

'I'm touched. Scott – that's his name? Scott and Tennyson. Do you get many jokes about that?'

He shook his head. 'I see you're a literary lady, Miss Aachen. Most of our customers are barely literate. "God in His mercy lent her grace." That's a lovely poem. Though I'd welcome your opinion on Lancelot. A bit shallow, he seems to me.'

'I don't want you to think I hate the police. My father was in the force.'

'Really? Where?'

'Dorking,' I said. It was the first place that came into my head. I couldn't tell him the truth.

He scratched his wiry hair. 'Dorking. Scott lives in Epsom, that's on the way there. The only thing I know about the Dorking police is that E. M. Forster had a long-standing affair with a policeman there.'

'No!' I said. The word kept coming 'No. *No*. NO. He couldn't be. No. No.'

Tennyson took the tissue and wiped the tears off my cheek. 'I thought a literary lady like you would know he was homosexual. Had to keep quiet about it while he was alive, but he's been dead—'

I couldn't stop it coming, 'No. No. No. No,' like bubbles breaking in my mouth.

I ran off to the ladies' to wash my face.

When I returned, he was standing up to go.

'I'm sorry,' I said. 'I'm just a bit overwrought.'

'I know. It can get you in funny ways. Your father?'

'Dead,' I said. 'He . . . died. A long time ago.'

'It can still hurt, even after all the years. Good night, Miss Aachen, I'm sure you'll be all right.'

I wasn't sure at all.

jangled

'He agreed with you about the lock,' I told Evian. She'd come up a couple of minutes after the policeman had gone, which told me something. 'He asked if you were a burglar.'

She cast her eyes up. 'With these nails?' She paused for a moment to admire them. 'Oh, someone from Customs and Excise called while you were out. I think it was about that Columbian cocaine.'

'Not funny,' I said. 'It'll be about my VAT returns. I wish I'd never bothered registering. I'm never going to earn enough to make it worthwhile. Especially when I'm tied up with this Rusty business.'

She fiddled with the pencils on my desk. 'How are you getting on?' she asked, too casually.

'Evian, I'm lost. I don't know what I'm doing. I think I'll give up.'

I watched her carefully.

'Probably for the best,' she said. 'I'll take the ring back, then.' Too quick.

'No, I've got to do it in person. I'm responsible. I'll have to give it into the hands of the rightful owner.'

She didn't say anything. She dug the pencil point into my blotter.

'Funny how one feels one's desk needs a blotter,' I said. 'I rarely use an ink pen these days. Of course, it's a moot point who is the rightful owner.'

She was drawing little circles, edges touching.

'I suppose really I ought to give it back to John.'

'Why?' She looked horrified. 'If you can't find Rusty, then it should go to Chantal.'

'Hardly,' I said. 'One doesn't give the ring one was given by one lover to the next one down the line. It isn't the pox, you know.'

'Cow.'

'I beg your pardon, Evian, I don't think I heard that.'

She pressed hard and broke the point off my HB pencil. 'This is just to wind me up.'

'You know, the lead in a pencil isn't lead. It's graphite, a mineral form of carbon. Like diamonds, only not so pretty. And a perfect ruby is worth more weight for weight than a diamond. My mother could tell you all about it. She used to teach geography, geology, that sort of thing. Why would I want to wind you up, Evian?'

'Because you think it's funny dangling thousands of pounds' worth of jewellery under my nose when I've got nothing, and threatening to give it to some rich bastard who—'

'Knows better than to spend it on gear? I'm not dangling it. It's in my safe.'

Her eyes flashed over to the safe.

'My inspector, as well as warning me about the door-locks, said the safe was very safe. Modern manufacture. You can't do tricks with tumblers and whatnots with these new safes. Of course, a professional with the right equipment could get into it eventually, but it wouldn't be worth the bother. These chaps come very expensive.'

Evian collapsed on to her folded arms. She lifted her head and her lip trembled. 'Hallie, why are you being like this? I only—'

'Don't. Don't dare shed a tear in this office.'

She stared at me open-mouthed.

'I have had enough, Evian. I'm tired of people manipulating my emotions. I feel jangled and mangled. A bit of fear here, a bit of guilt, a bit of—'

'The other?'

I couldn't help myself: I laughed. 'Evian, you don't know how close you got. I really am tired of it. I was considering giving it up, anyway. I don't suppose Rusty left a will?'

She didn't need to answer.

'I suppose it should go to her son. I don't know what the legal position is in these cases.'

Evian just sagged. I did feel a bit sorry for her.

'You didn't know the ring was valuable till after you gave it to me, did you?'

She shook her head. 'I knew what it was worth but . . .'

'You wouldn't have got much for it if you'd tried to sell it. That's its insurance value.'

'They would have thought I nicked it. But a respectable person like you would have to have insurance.' She perked up.

'Of course. I had to write to my insurers detailing it separately. It's over my limit.'

She didn't say anything, but her eyes moved in small slow circles from the blotter to the safe.

'Don't even think of it,' I said.

'We tried. That was the original idea. When Rusty left, Chantal asked me to sell the ring. But nobody would give me anything like its real value. So we thought of you. New office, insurance.'

'You were going to steal it back and get Muggins here to claim on her insurance? Apart from the ethics of it, what do you think it would have done to my premiums?'

72

'So that's it, then?'

I nodded. 'I'll finish the job, tie up the loose ends. I'll talk to one of my legal friends about probate.'

She stared at me, blank.

'That's about her will, her estate,' I explained.

'I know that. Do you really think it's her?'

'No, I think she went off with the boy to make a new life for them both. Evian, five minutes ago all you were interested in was getting your hands on the ring. Now that looks less likely, you've suddenly come over all "bereaved friend". I'm not buying it.'

She picked at a chip of nail polish, then peeled the whole nail off. 'Bugger. I can never manage to grow that one. Shall I tell you the truth, Hallie? I am upset. Really upset. That's why I need the gear. Of course I was going to snaffle the ring if I could, but that doesn't mean I don't care. Rusty was my friend. What if that was her? She didn't deserve to die like that, all chopped up.'

'Nobody deserves to die like that. But what can I do? I think it's a matter for the police. I'm not equipped for it.'

'Why did you take it on, then?'

'I didn't know it would get to me. Some of the things I've done in the last week have made me ill. It's bringing up too many things from the past. I took on a job of finding someone. I've done that before. I have all the contacts in all the agencies. I thought I could cope. I was wrong. But I committed myself and I will finish the job. That job doesn't include finding a killer, though.'

'Have you thought they might try to find you? That black car's back.'

the lover

John Deerhart was at his office.

'He's just eating a sandwich. I'll buzz him. He'll be along in a minute.'

I couldn't see her lasting. 'How long have you worked there, er, Miss . . . ?'

'Karen. About three months. Mr Deerhart's nice. He doesn't shout at me like my old boss. Are you a friend of his?'

'In a manner of speaking.'

'You never can tell with ladies, can you? Oh, here he is now.'

The voice changed. 'Deerhart.'

'Haydon Aachen. We met last—'

'Thank you, Ms Aachen. I have a very clear memory of our last meeting. Especially of your final words. Very distinct. I hardly think we have anything further to say to each other.' His voice sounded different over the phone, cold and crisp.

'Mr Deerhart, I do want to speak to you further. You suggested lunch.'

'That was before you made that unpleasant suggestion. I don't think—'

'Mr Deerhart, a woman's torso has been found in a Surrey wood.'

'I fail to see what . . . A what? You . . . Oh, God.' There

was a thump, the sound of the phone knocking on something hard, then Karen's voice, 'Oh, Mr Deerhart! Let me get you a chair. Water. Oh.'

I cursed myself for giving it to him over the phone. There was no way now I could judge if his reaction was genuine.

Eventually Karen came back on the line.

'I'm sorry,' I said. 'I've given him a bit of a shock. Just keep him there. I'll be over within half an hour.'

Deerhart had recovered by the time I arrived there. He met me as I stepped out of the lift.

'We have a table at the Shah Jehan. It's a pleasant place and has the advantage of being badly lit. In case you want to spring any more of your little surprises, I would rather be seated and out of the public glare.'

I was impressed that he'd got a table so quickly. I'd read about the Shah Jehan but never eaten there. I said, 'I thought you'd eaten already. How was your sandwich?'

'Karen is rather garrulous. Don't make the mistake of thinking she's stupid.'

We were seated at a small corner table behind a tall real palm. I wondered if John Deerhart had asked for it specially. It had two cloths of pink damask and matching napkins. The silver was heavy and gleaming. He arranged his napkin tenderly like a child tucking up a doll.

'Mr Deerhart, I apologize for the manner in which I broke that news to you.'

He steepled his fingers and looked at me over his pale elegant nails. 'You clearly think it is Rusty. Have you any grounds for that belief?'

He was too composed. I'd missed whatever opportunity there was of benefiting from his shock.

'No,' I said. 'Except for the timing. She hadn't been there longer than a week.'

'A week. I sup—' The waiter came. He suggested the special tray of mixed starters and Indian beer. Deerhart looked over at me.

'That sounds fine, but I'd rather have water, or wine.'

'Their house white OK?' Deerhart asked. 'It's a Sauvignon Blanc – dry enough for you?'

That said something about his attitude to money: he wasn't interested in showing off. At least not to me.

'Mr Deerhart, you were about to say something just now.'

'It was not a very pleasant thought. You know, you can call me John if you refrain from accusing me of murder.'

I have him! 'I'd like to hear the thought. John.'

'I was thinking even after a week there would be some . . . changes to the body.'

I choked and he called the waiter over with some water. 'Thank you. Sorry. Until you said that I'd been thinking of it like a piece of statuary. Venus de Milo. Not a flesh-and-blood woman.'

He took a gulp of water. 'I have the advantage there. I can recall Rusty's body. Every inch of it. Her skin. It was a lot like marble, pale. But soft like a flower petal and cool. She always felt slightly cold and damp to the touch. That sounds horrible. It wasn't, though. She was like a stem freshly plucked from the earth. Did you say it was in a wood?'

He mopped his face with the napkin, then rested it in his hands. A waiter slid up with the wine. I nodded for him to just pour and go.

I reached for Deerhart's hands, pulled them away from his face. 'Mr Deerhart, John, I know this is painful but, please, try to tell me about her, about your relationship. Talking will make you feel better.'

This was what I was good at.

His hand closed round mine. 'You didn't really believe I'd hurt her, Haydon?'

My stomach gave a little squeeze. I knew it of old: a mixture of dread and excitement. Someone's life was about to spill out before me and I, with a surgeon's precision, would pick out the pieces, slightly alter their alignment and hand them back. Then the person could go on and live their life. Not Rusty, though. Rusty's old life was over and done with. I hoped it wasn't in that shallow grave, that she'd gone to a better place.

'How did you meet her, John?'

The waiter arrived with a huge silver tray on which were crammed a dozen small silver dishes. He pointed them out. 'Prawn puri. Shashlik. Tikkas. Roti. Samosa. Pakora. Brinjal. Okra. Raita.'

'It's very corny. I ran into her in the street, knocked her bag out of her hand. It was full of weird things – that's what I thought then. I bought her a drink. I think I had some idea of saving her. I gave her my card and told her to contact me if she ever needed any help. I kept going back there. I was drawn to it, the squalor and the danger. I suppose I was the White Knight.'

'Did you tell her you wanted to rescue her?'

'She wasn't interested. Don't think she was a victim. That was my mistake. She was tougher than that.' He looked down at his hand still clasped in my faintly stained one. 'That seems to be my fate. I end up with the tough ones.'

I turned his hand over, ran my finger along the length of his soft palm, as if his life story were written there in braille. That was definitely not in the counselling-skills repertoire. 'I'm sorry for thinking—'

'I know, Haydon.'

I sipped my wine. The bottle was nearly empty. I thought

about Rusty. What had she got out of him? Was it pride or stubbornness that prevented her from taking more from him? She could have been set up for life. He seemed eminently pliable to me.

'What are you thinking, Haydon?'

'I am thinking that desire, need, is like nitro-glycerine. Those who can handle it can blast their way into any locked safe. And those who can't, the rest of us, we should take care. I'm also thinking that we've ordered the most expensive item on the menu and not eaten a bite.'

He smiled. 'I didn't expect you to. See, I remember all those little things about you.'

'I don't usually.' I bit into the prawn.

The inside of his lips showed, mauvy-pink. 'Then we must do this again.'

dishes

John Deerhart disturbed me in a way I didn't like to think about. Not at all what my mother was hoping for. He reminded me of a heroin-addicted probation officer I once worked with. There was something raw, peeled, about him, like a shell-less crustacean or the new skin that grows under a burn.

I had enjoyed probing him, and I felt slightly disgusted with myself. I could see how detecting might become addictive, all that power to play with people's emotions. I would do well to heed my own warning.

That only left Chantal. I'd put her off till last because I didn't know what to say. I was still furious that they'd tried to pull that scam on me. Worse, how could she let me think that Rusty was in danger when she knew all along she'd gone off with someone else? She was just a calculating little junkie, stringing me along for her next hit.

I was ready to give her a piece of my mind.

The place was a tip. I could smell it going up the stairs. It must be bad for business. Chantal opened the door and I wondered if it could be the same woman.

'You.' She smiled, but it was the tight grimace a mortician's hand makes on the face of a corpse. 'Any news?'

My instinct was to run. I'd misjudged her: I was way out.

Then my second nature, professional, took over. 'I think you should sit down, Chantal. Shall I make us some tea?'

79

She sat, angled at the middle like a torn paper kite. 'She's dead.' It wasn't a question.

'I'll make the tea.'

The sink was the source of one of the smells in the room. It was half full of stagnant greasy water and dishes. I let out the water. A slimy cloth hugged the plug-hole. I dropped it in the bin under the sink, disturbing a cloud of small flies. That was the second smell. I tied up the bag and put it out on the landing. I sloshed bleach round the sink and used the first kettle of water to wash the dishes.

Eventually I brought a cup of tea over to Chantal. She still sat in the position in which she'd dropped. I held it out to her. 'Drink it, Chantal. I know you don't want to do anything, but you can't live like this.'

She didn't move.

I reached out to place her hands round the cup. I touched her skin. It was clammy like a poisoned fish that has floated dead in the water. Soft. I felt she might just disintegrate in my fingers. I put the tea down.

'Chantal, someone, a body, a woman has been found in a wood. We don't know if it's Rusty. Chantal!'

Her eyes moved ever so slowly in my direction, then dropped as if the effort were too much. Her arms hung like white straws. Blue needle marks and white line scars glowed like luminous ink.

'Chantal, if it is Rusty . . .' I couldn't say my prepared speech. 'Well, that's it, then.'

'He said she knew him. He knew him. That's why he didn't stick around. She went with him.' Chantal shook her head, as if it was just too hard to collect her thoughts.

'What are you saying, Chantal? Who knew who?'

'No, it's gone. She's gone. It doesn't make any difference now.'

'Chantal, please!'

'No. She's gone. Too late. Not worth his life as well.'

She didn't look at me again. I didn't feel I could leave without some dismissal on her part. I flapped around, making no real dent in the filth and chaos. I found a cardigan in the bedroom. I wrapped it round her bare shoulders. The tea was still untouched.

'Chantal, I'll have to go. I'll see if I can get somebody round to help. If you do decide you want to talk, you know how to get hold of me.'

A fat bluebottle flew close to her face. She blinked. I took that as acknowledgement and left.

night visit

I sat in the office for a long time, letting the evening fall round me. When it got too dark to see my hand, I turned on the light. I was too exhausted to move, but I couldn't face another night on the camp bed with the springs and the cold and no clean clothes.

I decided to review my progress so far, sum up and then close the case for the night. That's what they told you to do in all the best time-management books.

Aim: find Rusty.

As soon as I listed Resources and Obstacles, my problem leapt out at me. The lists were the same: police, Evian, Chantal, Billie, Deerhart.

The police treated me like an hysterical woman. I sensed they were covering up for Grazeley. Tennyson didn't fool me: he was being helpful in order to keep an eye on me.

I didn't know what Evian's game was but she'd do anything for money. I wasn't sure I believed in the black car. She was the only one who'd seen it.

Chantal made no sense. If she knew Rusty was planning to leave and the ruby scam was her insurance as jilted lover, why was she now convinced that something had happened to Rusty? Who had she been going to meet that night? Was Chantal saying she knew him?

Billie was hiding. He didn't need to be hiding from

anybody. He had a history of running away. The rest could as easily be street paranoia. Bernie had hinted as much.

And Deerhart? Could anyone be as soft as he appeared to be?

I thought of another approach: consequences. I drew a flow chart.

If the body in Surrey was not Rusty's, then I could: (a) give up (end of line), after all it wasn't a *bona fide* commission. Evian had made that clear; (b) continue the search (branch B). Lots of sub-branches came off B, corresponding to the various leads.

I turned my attention to the other possibility. If it was Rusty, I could legitimately close the case: she'd been found.

Who was I kidding? She'd been found with her limbs and head cut off. Someone had done that to her, someone whose path I may have crossed in the course of my search, someone who might not like me asking questions. I'd been warned off directly at the clubs, and indirectly. Perhaps I should take the hint.

I knew nothing that the police didn't know already. I suspected they knew a good deal more than they let on and that my recent encounters were connected to my interest in Rusty.

Even if I decided to go after the killer, I wouldn't know how to go about it. I just had to let him know that. Or her, but that seemed unlikely.

I'd told Evian I was giving up. I just had to tell everyone else and watch their reactions. Evian would tell Chantal and then all the girls would know. I could phone Deerhart in the morning. No, get it over with now.

'Christine Deerhart.'

What was it about her voice? She didn't have the same accent as Carole, but something in her phone manner woke all my long-buried memories. It was the way she breathed: a short intake then a long time before she released it. I knew that breathing as well as I knew my own. The tone and the diction carried conflicting messages, like Lady Bracknell purring, 'Come to bed.' A dangerous demand to deal with.

'Hello, is John home yet?' I didn't want her sending me round to the tradesmen's entrance.

'No, I should think he's making his way home now. Who is calling?'

'Haydon Aachen.'

'Not a name one would forget. You intrigue me. My husband is always rather ruffled after meeting with you.' Her emphasis on the American form 'with' was both ironic and disapproving.

'It's about some business we had together. Tell him I'm probably closing the case. If what we talked about is what we thought it might be, then that's me finished.'

She repeated it verbatim, but with a little trill of incredulity. 'That's the message?'

I said I'd be in the office for a bit, or he could ring me in the morning. I regretted it almost as soon as I put the phone down. I wanted a drink. I didn't want to wait for a phone call. I decided to pop out to the pub across the road and finish my list later.

The Marquis was bursting at the seams, even the pavement outside was full. First bit of warm weather. The Crown where Evian had taken me was huge and the downstairs bar would be open. It was worth the walk to get a seat.

One drink turned into two and it looked like I'd be there all night. It wasn't my willpower that got me moving. A drunk in a red shirt had pawed me twice on his way to the gents'. Because I hadn't broken his arm, on his way back the third time he sat down next to me. He swung a hand in my vague direction. My drink went over. I didn't wait to be mopped dry. I swore at him and went back to my office.

A black car sped past, splashing me, as I ducked into the little cobbled alley. It reminded me of Evian's warning. Nobody would jump me on busy, lit streets, but here was the perfect place. There were pools of shadow where the street-lamps didn't reach. The drains were clogged and yesterday's rain lay still in the gutter. I imagined blood spilt there lying undetected for days.

On either side, blank, eyeless windows reflected themselves endlessly. Light leaked from behind my blinds, fell on the opposing glass, returned fainter like a message. I stood for a long time on the corner where the light met the dark, hesitating before I plur.ged.

Then I remembered. It wasn't a visual memory but an echo of muscle and tendon: left wrist extended, click down, withdrawn; right wrist twisted, thumb pressing, the push and turn of a stiff lock. Because I felt it in my fingers, along the back of my hands, my forearms, I knew it wasn't an illusion. I had switched off the main light before locking the door. First I'd turned off the desk light, then the main light and left the office in darkness.

The knowledge travelled up my elbows, upper arms, shoulders. It froze and pivoted me, and swung me back like a marionette. I wanted to run and I wanted to stay. I could turn and walk away: the worst that could happen would be my typewriter filched.

I stood transfixed by the fuzzy square of light that crossed and re-crossed the alley. Why would burglars turn on the light? It would attract attention; they were used to working in the dark, by torchlight. Were they sitting there waiting, the men? Whose men?

Did they want to talk, to persuade? Could I convince

them I had already given up? I tried to recall how far I'd got with my flow-chart. What would somebody reading it conclude? There were two convincing 'Give up' boxes, but what about the rest?

I stood till my legs were stiff and the cold threatened to immobilize me permanently. I knew my only hope of persuading them I had given up was to talk to them. I knew. I was afraid. If I turned round and left them to it, they would come after me. Sooner or later we would meet. I had to face them: I was scared to.

There was no movement, no shadows thrown. They were sitting calmly waiting for me. One, maybe the boss, would be sitting in my chair, his face in shadow. I'd seen the films. They wouldn't do anything to me if I could assure them I'd dropped the case. I would be safe then. So why didn't I do it, go up there?

I could stand here all night and die of pneumonia. That'd show them.

I took the stairs carefully, silently. Maybe I could listen at the door. My own door! Anger took me up the last steps. How dare they? I flung open the door.

There was someone in my chair. I couldn't see the face. The head was slumped forward on my desk, the fingers splayed across my papers. I didn't need to see the face. I recognized the tousled hair and the dusty bomber jacket.

giving up

The pulse, H., check the pulse. My first-aid training came back to me in drips. Neck is more reliable than wrist. Just to the side of the wind-pipe. Don't press too hard, and never both sides at once.

I pushed back the hair. I didn't need to find the pulse. She was warm and breathing.

'Phoo, you gave me a shock. I thought you were dead.'

'Dead?' She opened one eye. 'Dead?'

'What are you doing in my office?'

She shook her head and pulled her face between her hands. 'Sleeping, it looks like.'

'I see you've been going through my notes. Not enough in there to keep you awake?'

'I didn't get any sleep last night.'

'You wouldn't be much use as a guard dog then.'

That woke her up. 'Please. I won't fall asleep again.'

Her face was pale under the grime. She was undersized but not thin. She looked as if she lived on burgers and doughnuts. I felt a terrible need to trust someone.

'If I let you stay here, you've got to wash. There's a shower down the corridor. I'm not having you stink this place out.'

She nodded.

'Do you have a change of clothes?'

She shook her head.

'I'll get you some in the morning. And I'll talk to someone I know about getting you permanent accommodation.'

She screwed up her face.

'You're eighteen, they're not going to put you anywhere you don't want to go. We'll talk about it in the morning. I'll tell you what I want from you in exchange.'

She straightened her shoulders and pushed out her chin.

'Now I don't want any heroics. Simply by being here you'll put off most burglars. If anyone does break in while you're here, you know nothing about me, you just broke in yourself for somewhere warm to sleep. Got that?'

She nodded. She was glowing.

'What did you make of my notes, anyway?' I tried to sound light, casual, as if this wasn't what I'd been building up to since I'd found her here.

She shook her head. 'I didn't really understand them. Seemed a bit like one of those adventure game stories. You know, if you would take the forest road, turn to page thirty-seven.'

'And which road would you take? No, which road do you think I would take?'

Her little brown button eyes fixed on my face. Don't assume, H., because someone is young they can't see through you.

'I think you're fed up with it all. Your friends aren't any help and there are . . .' she scratched her head, recalling my exact word, '. . . obstacles in your way. But you're too kind to give up.'

'Kind?' I was speechless.

She dropped her eyes. 'Well, maybe that's the wrong word. But, you know . . .'

She reached for my hand.

I remembered the scars and pulled back. 'Bernie, one thing. If you're going to use this office, no physical stuff. Of any description.'

'Yes, boss.' She grinned.

I showed her where everything was, repeated my instructions, and then left for my own comfortable bed.

It was only outside, in the wind, when I felt the cold on my cheeks, that I knew I was crying. Bernie was right. I couldn't give up.

I wanted everyone to know I was giving up.

Karen answered at Deerhart's office. 'Is that Haydon Aachen? Mr Deerhart said he was expecting a call and to keep you on the line until he could be reached. Hang on.' There were various clicks and buzzes. 'He's coming now. This is exciting. He doesn't even say that for his wife. You did know he had a wife?'

'Of course.'

I thought I heard a faint hum of disappointment, but it could have been the line.

'Yes, a very nice wife, Mrs Deerhart, very glamorous. But then you're quite, um, striking, Miss Aachen.'

'Indeed. I'm sure Mr Deerhart's interest in me is purely business, so my appearance is neither here nor there.'

'I'm sure.' She giggled. 'Here he is now.'

John Deerhart had got my message, but still insisted he needed to talk to me. Maybe Karen was right. I said I was busy for lunch. We agreed to meet at five, at the NY Diner which was very quiet at that hour.

After I put the phone down, I thought about Christine Deerhart's remark. Mine wasn't a name to forget. I'd just assumed she meant it was unusual. I'd picked it for that very purpose. Maybe she meant something else. I felt peculiar, shivery.

Mirroring other people, reflecting back their words, had become second nature. I forgot there was a me behind the reflection that people reacted to. I realized I didn't know how people saw me. I had probably crossed one boundary too many with John Deerhart. Don't mix alcohol and business, I of all people should know that.

I wrote a note for Grazeley:

> Mr Grazeley,
> A woman's body has been found in Surrey. If this is identified as Rusty's, I will consider my commission to locate her has been fulfilled and will never need to visit any of your establishments again.

I enclosed my card. I debated whether to append some ironic comment about the pleasure of his company, but decided it would only invite a reply. I left the note with one of his minions, and told him to make sure Mr Grazeley got it.

I left a message for Inspector Tennyson, thanking him for his advice and asking what progress had been made with the identification.

christine

Getting Bernie housed kept my mind off Rusty. Here was something I could do. I knew the magic words. I was tired of failing and feeling used. Even though it was my own fault. I jumped too quickly to conclusions. Not every slumped body is dead. And the corpse may not be anyone you know.

'Is it all right to say you're a lesbian?' I asked her.

'Sure. Is it a problem?'

'No, quite the opposite. Just checking.'

She came over and sat on my desk. 'It is a problem.'

'No.' I didn't want to look at her.

'It's a problem for you. Look, you jump every time I go anywhere near you.'

'It's not that.' I moved my chair back.

'I'm eighteen.'

'I suppose that's part of it.' I forced myself to look at her. Her squashed nose and monkey mouth made her look in some ways like a new-born baby. 'You're eighteen, how can you be so sure? I'm twice your age and I haven't worked it out yet.'

I could tell by the little smile and the droop of the eyelid that she thought this was one of those tall tales that grown-ups tell. She'd listen but she wouldn't believe it for a minute.

'All right, off the desk.'

I picked up the phone and dialled. 'Jay, hi. Haydon. Are

your lists open? Listen, I've got an eighteen-year-old young woman here, lesbian, sleeping rough, has been in care . . . Great, yes, I'll try them.'

By the end of the morning I had two interviews set up for Bernie. She had several pencil sketches of me.

'I like that one,' I said pointing. 'You've really got my jaw. Like granite. Makes me think of those Russian statues of the thirties.'

She looked puzzled. 'Are you a communist, then?'

I didn't know how to reply. 'Well, I suppose I can't be now. I've got my own business. Private enterprise. I do believe in the welfare state. I just couldn't stand working for it. It was like a disaster movie, everyone just hanging on for the final collapse. Nobody was going to rescue us. What about you? Do you have any politics?'

'Anarchist. "Class War". That kind of thing. But I do agree with the Tories about the sanctity of the family.'

'You what?' Calm down, Haydon, she's spent most of her life in institutions. Some people have God, some people Father Christmas, she believes in Family Life.

'Yes, I don't think you should have children outside marriage.'

'But you're—'

'I don't think lesbians should have children.'

Before I could get any further the phone rang. It was Christine Deerhart.

'Miss Aachen, I wonder if you'd like to come over for drinks?'

For an instant, again, my body processes seemed to stop: breath, blood, all my senses, were silent. Carole. No, not her. Her voice was deeper.

I agreed to see her. She was becoming, in my imagination,

larger than life: I needed to cut her down to her rightful size.

She didn't seem surprised that I knew the address, and cut through my faffing about directions with a promise to send a car to pick me up from the station. 'Miss Aachen, you don't know what pleasure it gives me to anticipate your visit.'

I was trembling when I put the phone down. 'That woman terrifies me,' I told Bernie. 'She's reduced me to jelly in a couple of sentences.'

I phoned my mother to check points of etiquette.

'You're sure it's drinks and no dinner? Interesting. No other guests?' I could imagine her consulting a little linen-covered book she kept for these occasions.

'What shall I wear, Mother?'

'Do you have a little cocktail frock? Not full-length that early in the evening. Not your working clothes, though. That's terribly *petit bourgeois*. Sensible suit with camisole just reeks of trade.'

'Mother, there's only me here. You don't have to impress.'

'Darling, one's only audience is oneself, and one does have to impress oneself. Absolutely.'

'And what does one drink, Mother?'

'Pimms if it's outside. Or . . . you're not a gin drinker, are you?'

'No, whiskey.'

'Not that, darling. Too masculine. Oh, just some sort of cocktail. Manhattan. Martini. Nothing whose name suggests fornication, though.'

'Thanks, Mother. I'll give you a run-down of the house afterwards, curtains, furniture, everything.'

'And, darling, you must get yourself a decent pair of court shoes.'

None of my wardrobes would furnish me with a little cocktail frock. There was an enormous indigo taffeta creation that made me look like a Zeppelin in drag. There were several sequined sparkly things, but none of them fitted. I thought I had it with a clinging black velour number until I saw the arrow-shaped scorch mark on the hem. Who were these people who ironed velvet frocks?

I turned to my collection of day dresses. *Petit bourgeois* it might be, but I'd have to settle for it. I ran my fingers along the hangers until they were stopped by the familiar dry rustle of silk.

'What's it to be, then?'

I pulled it out. They called them tea dresses. It was a drop-waisted, front-buttoning, three-quarter-sleeved affair in black silk crêpe-de-Chine with a tiny white geometric pattern that might have been fleurs-de-lys or peace doves. The buttons were self-covered, which was a weakness of mine. I was glad of the pattern. It would have looked a little too much like mourning otherwise.

the ideal husband

John Deerhart's face lit up as I came in. My stomach rose to meet my mouth. Two serious errors in one day. I loathed my own obtuseness. I am a big strong woman, I told myself, I'll play it as it is dealt.

He stood, held his arms out and kissed me lightly on the cheek.

'What would you like to drink, Haydon? They have an excellent selection of beers, but you're not very keen as I remember.'

'Whiskey and soda, light on the soda.' My mother would die.

I watched him go to the bar. He moved neatly like a dancer. He was wearing a lightweight grey-blue suit. His hair was well cut, thinning but healthy, kempt. He wore his money lightly, and he didn't smell. That was important. Aftershave made me gag. As for the other male smells, I didn't even want to think about them. I tried to imagine him undressed. I didn't get very far. His body hair would be fine, pale and sleek as a mouse's.

John Deerhart was just the kind of man my mother would like me to marry. A pity that the disturbing Christine had got there first. I had a sudden vision of her dropping him before me like a mouse-present, batting him with a paw. It was Carole's green cat eyes I saw.

'Haydon, you're miles away. What are you thinking?'

'I was actually thinking about your wife. Karen was very keen to let me know you were married.'

He didn't look uncomfortable. I liked that about him. 'Karen tries to protect me. From unscrupulous women.' He smiled at me over his beer.

'A sort of chattering chastity belt?'

'Take care, Haydon, you sound the teeniest bit bitchy.'

You smug pig. You really believe I want you. 'It must be jealousy. So Karen wants you all to herself?'

'No, she likes my wife. A lot of women do. She has a way of making an impression.'

'How vulgar. I thought one was supposed to leave that sort of thing to dentists.'

He looked up sharply. There was froth on his upper lip. 'You sounded just like her for a moment.'

Another Oscar Wilde fan. I was beginning to like her a lot better than the ideal husband.

'Oh dear, John. This conversation is going quite queer. Here I am, reminding you of your wife, fending off your secretary, hardly the best way to start an affair.'

'She's not mine, we share her. An affair, did you say?'

'I take it you mean Karen, not your wife. That would be too liberal. Yes, I did say an affair. Isn't that what this is all about?'

He blushed, a real pink spreader, like wine soaking into a white table-cloth. 'Oh, Haydon. I don't . . . Well, yes, I mean no. I . . .'

I found it curiously exciting. I hadn't flirted, if that's what this was, with a man for years. I felt powerful. 'It was that gesture, the way you held your arms as I came over, that kiss that said next time it will be on the lips. And now I've blown it. You'll never be able to say: my wife doesn't understand me.'

96

He sat up higher in his stool. The pink was fading prettily. 'I never have said it. She understands me perfectly. You're labouring under the same misapprehension as Karen. I don't cheat on my wife. There's no deception involved.'

I swirled my ice-cubes. 'How frightfully aristocratic. And me only just made it to the middle classes.'

'You do sound like her.' He glanced down at his beer. He looked both wistful and expectant.

For a second I had a flash of what it had been like between him and Rusty. I felt a fierce desire – not for his body: it was impossible to imagine him naked – to torment him. There would be a joy in seeing his pretty hands plead, his sensitive face pucker. There was a small spoilable beauty to him.

'John,' I said, carefully because I didn't like the person I was becoming here, 'I am wondering how you can think of finding someone else . . . to fuck . . . [he winced] . . . when it might be Rusty in that shallow grave.'

'You forget, she ended it months ago. I've had a long time to get used to her not being around.'

I wanted to throw my drink at him, grind the glass in his face. I just gripped it, and said sweetly, 'Of course, that must be it. Do you know who I went to see today, John?'

He shook his head. His eyes never left my face. I had the feeling they could see right through me.

'I went to see a prostitute.'

He didn't move.

'She was Rusty's lover, she loved her. She has more holes in her arms than in her fishnets. She hasn't got used to it. She's eaten up with grief. It's stripped the flesh off her. She's like a skeleton. She can't work. She can't fuck. And you, you're not fit to—' I jumped up, banged a note down on the table. 'For the drink.'

He caught my hand, held it to the table. 'Haydon.' I could have broken his grip but his eyes held me. They stung mine like onion with their rawness. 'Haydon. Don't.'

I subsided back into my chair. 'I know. It's not real.'

'You really think it's her now?'

'I don't know. Seeing Chantal shook me. They lied to me, they set me up, but now they're acting like she is dead. I don't know what to think.' I turned away so he wouldn't see my eyes screw up.

'You're not really like my wife,' he said.

I knew what he was going to say next, but it didn't stop the lurch in my stomach when he did say it. 'You're like me. You hide it better than me. That's all. The guilt and the terror. I'm right, aren't I, Haydon?'

I wanted to throw myself into his arms, to cry and be comforted and protected. I knew I couldn't. He was weak. We couldn't hold each other up. I tried for a joke instead. 'Tell me about your wife. Is she really grand and impressive? Like an opera house?'

'Not really. She's slim and very fit. She rides.'

'Of course. She would.' For a second I saw a gilded Amazon astride his pale body, teeth and green eyes flashing. 'Does she hunt?'

'Not creatures.' He smiled. 'She can. She works part of the week in a gunsmiths'-cum-estate-agent. She looks very elegant with a twelve-bore.'

My mouth went dry. The body in the wood virtually on their doorstep. What had Chantal said: She knew him, that's why she went? She? He? 'Oh?' I croaked.

He didn't pick up on my change of mood. 'Yes, it's very common round our way. The indoorsy types run antiques and interior-decoration businesses. The others are into guns, land and horseflesh.'

Guns, horseflesh, butchery. I made the effort to sound light. 'My mother will be sad.'

'I beg your pardon?'

'She always wanted me to marry someone like you.'

He touched just the tips of my fingers.

'Come on, John. Say it.' My heart wasn't in it, but I kept going.

'Say what?'

'Will you marry me? Let me take you away from all this. I'm sure your wife won't mind. She's very understanding.' I gave a little laugh and dug my knuckles into my eyes.

'Haydon, please.' He'd lost it. The beer kept slopping out of his glass on to the beer mat. He couldn't manage to get it to his mouth.

Take advantage of his bewilderment. 'Did you ever ask Rusty to marry you? Did your wife mind?'

'No, and no.'

'Do you think that's why she dumped you? None of us likes to be second best. Chantal loved her, and you were just playing games. That's what married people do, fool around.'

He opened his mouth to say something. All that came out was a sigh.

I caught the side of his mouth with my fingers. It was such a sad sound. I breathed it in and felt it going to that deep place below the stomach where all the sad things lie. So that was the end of the affair. Before it had even begun. Kissing would seem crude now. I touched his cheek and left.

woman with a gun

My mother was right about the shoes, but I couldn't be bothered shopping. The Italian kid slippers would have to do.

It was a terrible time to take a commuter train. Old hands had bagged not only the seats but the elbow-rests for standing passengers while I was still checking the indicator board. It was a non-stopping train, fast but no chance of a seat before Dorking.

The dress was already wilting, but I appreciated my mother's snobbery about business suits. My fellow passengers, male and female, looked infinitely more wretched in their suits than I felt. I smirked into the back of their newspapers.

Football and tennis, neither of which interested me. It is too easy to develop the body at the expense of the mind: that was my excuse. I imagined Christine Deerhart would play tennis when she wasn't in the saddle. She'd have a suntan that went all the way up to her buttocks and a strong forearm. I knew that forearm. I was shocked by the drivel running through my head. What had got into me? Surely there was a *Financial Times* amongst this lot. But that was morning reading. And I bet all the crosswords were filled in.

I was so hot and irritable that I didn't bother with tights when I got off the train. I walked straight out through the arched station forecourt into the dry, seed-laden air.

'Miss Aachen?'

I didn't know how he picked me out from all the commuters, maybe the lack of a suit. He had the car fan on blowing cold. Already I could feel my eyes turn pink and tiny allergic reactions explode in my nostrils. I didn't see much of the countryside we passed through except to note it was green. The windscreen was spattered with tiny leaves and seeds and resinous blobs.

At some point we'd turned off into an unmade road. We passed a field of something yellow; its brightness stung my eyes. I was thinking this was what my mother aspired to, small and neat and dull. Nothing happens in the English countryside. Then someone pointed a gun at us.

I giggled. The driver ignored it. It wasn't pointed directly at us. The holder was a woman; I couldn't see much else. She was wearing one of those tweed jackets that survived the last Ice Age and is still going strong. Her hair was covered by a red and gold scarf. She appeared to be doing an English gentlewoman's version of *tai chi*. She swivelled slowly, sighting along the horizon, then up in an arc to the zenith and down again.

I didn't know what to make of it. I only saw her for a few seconds before she was hidden again by hedges. Could it have been Christine Deerhart? Even if it wasn't, did she also engage in this strange salute to the sun with a shotgun? It seemed as if I'd left behind my own bearings and entered a world of bizarre and unpredictable behaviour.

I should be on my guard. Maybe I was clutching at straws in believing Rusty had got on that train to a new life. It would only take one bullet. It didn't have to be Deerhart. A woman could use a gun as well as a man.

We bumped along through a tunnel of branches, then the car stopped and reversed down a walled lane. This ended in

101

a gate and a stone courtyard. My first view of Christine Deerhart was over the top of my handkerchief. I'd rummaged in my bag for antihistamines, but too late. I remembered why I didn't live in the country.

I stumbled out of the car. The driver took off back down the lane. Christine Deerhart shimmered before me. All I took in was that she was my height – not many women were – and that she was wearing something long and silvery. So much for my mother's 'not before nightfall'.

It was evening. The sky was a pinky mauve, and as she led me round the back of the house, she lit big pearly globes. They hung like extra moons against the darkening sky. As it grew violet, their light formed a halo of swirling silver gas.

'What can I get you to drink?'

I didn't want to appear unsophisticated, nor did I want her drawing conclusions from the fact that I usually drank whiskey before dinner.

'A dry martini?' I croaked.

She opened a cabinet and I saw three different bottles of aged malt including a very rare lowland. She mixed my martini then poured herself a large Macallan.

'I'll just get the ice.' She smiled, showing very even teeth. I ran my tongue over my own, tasting the forsworn whisky.

She flicked past me, her eelskin sheath-dress glittering like a start of small fishes. Carole, in diamonds. What had I got myself into?

I took a breath that I felt would inflate an airship and willed every cell in my body to be calm.

I tried to remind myself of the facts: this woman was a suspect; she suspected me of having an affair with her husband; her husband may have been implicated in Rusty's disappearance, even death; she might want to protect her husband or spite him. She was handy with a shotgun.

She reappeared with the ice. She wavered between real and unreal. It was a mistake to come here. All of it was a mistake. The drink. Everything. I eyed her iced whisky enviously. Beads of water were running down the outside, wetting her fingers. Her nails were cut square. Short. Not like her husband's delicate rodent fingers. She wore no ring.

I coughed. 'So, you wanted to see me?'

'Very to the point, Ms Aachen. I wanted to see you. You have been seeing a lot of my husband.'

She looked at me over the beaded tumbler.

I dropped my eyes. 'Not the way you mean. I have a job to do. I need his help.'

'Yes?' Her eyes didn't waver. Why did they have to be green? I knew this was a mistake.

I took a gulp of the martini. The fumes from the gin burnt my eyes. 'I'm not interested in your husband. I mean, I don't . . . I . . .'

The green eyes swept over my body. Evenly. Like radar.

I'd done one thing right at least. The black silk tea dress wasn't a mistake. She was armoured in silver chainmail. Pinched tight at the breast. Her ghostly hair floated about bare shoulders. In the light of the globes, she seemed almost metallic.

'Well, Ms Aachen. You were saying?'

I took a deep breath. 'I have no sexual interest in your husband. I . . .' The silk of my dress was hot against my back. I stared into the martini. There was a small green olive, unstoned, leaning against the triangular side.

She put her drink down on the small table.

'And?' She took the shaking glass from my hand. Her fingers were cold.

Her mouth was hot and cold and tasted of whisky.

103

pictures

Strange light. Greenish, bobbing with shadows like the under-surface of a pond. Odd dream. Sirens.

I opened my eyes to a strange room. The wallpaper was a watered down apple green – 'eau-de-Nil', in decorator's language – with a pale cream stripe so faint that you could only see it close to. I saw it through the polished cherrywood arch of a bed-head. The windows were draped in matching ruched blinds. The bed-cover was a bluer green – 'aqua'. I was pleased that it was not a perfect match.

My dress hung over the back of a bentwood chair. My shoes were under it, and my brassière was folded on the seat. Someone had put me to bed. I had a second's hallucination of sure square fingers unbuttoning me and heavy pale hair falling across my face. No, that was the dream.

I brushed away the dream hair. The fingers of my right hand were red to the knuckle. Oh, Sherlock.

There was a tap on the door. I hid the offending hand. Christine Deerhart came in with a cup of tea.

'Feeling any better?'

I had difficulty focusing on her. Something slipped between, like double glass. She was dressed for riding. Queen Christina. White short-sleeved lawn shirt, beige pants with a belt the exact same shade as the bed-head. The hair floated straight out of the dream.

She opened the blinds. Light flowed round her. The room

was brighter but still green. Summer leaves, shade on shade, waved in the window. Her shirt was like gauze with the light behind it. I gulped air against the mermaid outline of her breasts.

'No one's ever passed out on me like that before.' She laughed.

I clenched my hands tight under the cover. She sat down on the bed side-saddle, like a lady. I had to say something.

'It's my horm . . . histamones. I shouldn't drink. Reaction.' It was very hard to speak without my hands.

'I'll let you get dressed.'

No, touch me. I felt the bed rise slightly as she got up. I closed my eyes tight, waiting for it. It wasn't a dream last night. Please. I heard the snick of the door closing.

She was gone. I crawled out of bed to assess the damage. The fitted bottom sheet was more ice-blue than aqua. My mother had a word for it. Mortifying. One wet red puddle and a rusty smear.

There was a wash basin in the corner. I had my emergency kit and the unused tights in my bag. I made myself decent, then stripped the bed. Of course, it had soaked through to the mattress. No, I would not be joining Christine for breakfast.

I crept out the back way I had come in the night before, my Italian slippers in my hand. The stones of the lane were sharp on my feet but I'd decided to save my shoes at all costs.

I couldn't remember which way we'd turned into the lane but I gambled on left. I walked for almost an hour along the unmade road. My feet ceased to feel the individual cuts and bumps and became single hot pads of soreness. There should be a stream, somewhere to cool them off. The best I could manage was the grass under the trees which was soft and wetter than the brittle roadside tufts.

When I'd almost despaired of it, I came to the main road.

Left or right? I thought I ought to be going north. It was morning so the shadows should be pointing due west. Going clockwise, north should be a quarter turn from west. I turned a full circle then a bit more. I was pointing leftish. I had a fifty per cent chance of being right.

There should have been signposts. Or a phone-box. There wasn't much traffic for a dual carriageway. I thought about hitching, but what cars there were were going too fast. They wouldn't be likely to stop. Besides I wasn't desperate enough yet to take the risk. Maybe a taxi. This was somewhere near the airport, wasn't it? They queue up at the airport. They don't cruise up and down on the off-chance.

I sat down on the grass. Disgrace at the Deerharts' would have been preferable. I could go back. Look at it logically, H. It was highly unlikely I could walk for another hour along this road without coming to a town or a phone or a sign. I got up. By the shadows, I was now walking due east. If I walked for long enough I'd hit the sea.

I heard it before I saw it. A diesel engine. I'd been thinking of a cab. I turned. The roof of a bus showed over the low rise. I jumped and waved. Please. I was surprised when it stopped.

'You all right, love?'

It was a woman driver, sitting high in the cab, in a short-sleeved white shirt. There the resemblance to Christine ended. Still, I had to shake my head to make sure she was real.

'Has anything happened? I can radio in.' She was looking at me, worried.

A woman wandering, dusty, shoeless, eyes streaming, in the middle of nowhere. It must look odd. 'No, it's all right. Just hay fever. Where are you going?'

'Reigate.'

'Reigate's fine. Reigate's wonderful. North of Dorking.'

She'd already thumbed off a ticket and restarted the bus.

I wove my way to a seat.

'My mistake was heading north. Sometimes you have to go back to go forward,' I said to the startled woman beside me. 'I can get a bus from Reigate to my mother's.'

She smiled nervously.

I washed at Reigate and put on my tights. My mother's greeting was typical.

'Darling, what have you been up to? You look as though you've been rolling in the grass. It's a bit early in the day for frolics.'

'No such luck, Mother.'

'You've been to see those new friends of yours. Don't look like that. I know you wouldn't come to see me unless it was on the way back from something more interesting. Did it go well?'

'Don't ask. Disastrous. You don't want to know.'

'I don't.'

I touched my lips to her cheek. I smelt face powder and White Linen perfume. My mother describes her complexion as 'typical English rose' though the genes are Germanic. The texture of her skin I have never encountered on any other flesh. It is starched, powdery, matt, like fine table damask or old paper.

'Come in and change. That would be quite an attractive dress if it were ironed. It suits your colouring.'

This was said with a faint tut that may have been just her teeth slipping. My mother sees my colouring as a misfortune to be borne in stoic silence. Her hair is so subtly tinted that for many years I believed that blondes faded, like the gold

107

rim on old china, delicately to silver. So much about my mother is touched up, I no longer trust anything.

She found me a shirt and a pair of red trousers, short in the leg. When I offered to pay for the cleaning she gasped. 'I'm not senile yet. I can still wash and iron.'

I shrugged.

'Business, you said, darling. What was the business?'

'I have to find somebody,' I said.

'Oh?'

I took the photo of Wee Billie out of my bag and showed it to her. I must have been angry. I knew what the effect would be.

'Oh, my dear!' She sat down heavily.

'Shall I get you a drink?'

My mother liked to imply by gesture or tone of voice that it was a habit she picked up in the Raj. Indian tonic. One also inferred, by omission, that it was only tonic she drank. I thought as a child that the acrid fumes were quinine. I was shocked when I discovered otherwise.

'Just how you like it.' The smell made my head spin.

'Thank you, darling. It's the shock. He's so like—'

'He's alive,' I said. 'I want to see he stays that way.'

'Oh, darling.'

She took down the big maroon album. It was padded, the leather worn brown in places from handling. I sat with its weight on my lap. I flipped through the familiar pages. Their wedding: he in uniform, she in her austerity suit. Softer: a pastel silky dress flapping her knees in the sea wind. Then me. A square black-eyed baby in a vast trailing robe. Toddling in a blousy silk romper suit. My favourite: aged two or three on his lap, his dark hair and square jaw a laughing reflection of my own, a big and small mirror totally absorbed.

108

They stop suddenly at seven. There's no gap, just a jump-cut to aged eleven, formal, posed, a pudding-basin school hat squashed down over beetle brows. It's not me. A double brought in for some dark purpose. You can tell. None of the later ones smile.

I turn back to the last one of him. It is a self-conscious film-star pose. He holds on to a rail and gazes out to sea. In profile, the jaw is rugged, masculine; the eyes soft, woman-ish. In retrospect there is a hint in the stance: he could be contemplating going over the side. The grey sea has faded over the years to almost white. His eyes have grown cloudier as if full of coming storms.

'It's inside the back cover. I couldn't bear to look at it, or throw it away.'

My mother's voice pulled me back from the sea.

'I know.'

The end sheet is caught behind a plastic window. I slip out the photo. It is soft and furry at the edges. She could not bear to look at it, but she must have, hundreds of times over the years. I have seen it three times, but it is no surprise when I look at it. My memory of it is perfect.

The memory comes tagged with a phrase of my mother's: 'It's hereditary, you know, in the blood.'

He must have been on holiday. His hair is a shade too long. One dark lock curls an inverted question mark mid-forehead. His arm is round the boy's shoulder. To me he's never had a name, just 'the boy'. My father's smile is the same as in my favourite photo, intense, utterly absorbed. The boy looks up at him. His smile is uneven, one side slightly higher than the other. No wonder my mother needed the gin.

'Yes, it's an eerie likeness,' I told her.

It wasn't really. The boy in the photo was a young man,

nearly as tall as my father. Billie was a small fifteen, looked twelve. When I'd looked at the photo in my teens, trying to glare through the emulsion to the truth, I saw the boy as my big brother. That was the only sense I could make of it being 'in the blood'. I couldn't understand why that was so awful, even in the fifties.

He didn't look like a brother. He had a heart-shaped face and light brown hair. There was nothing about him that suggested we were related. Just the look. The way his gaze locked with my father's and blocked out the whole world. Not a father and son look.

'Well, Inspector Tennyson, was it a shot in the dark?' Then it hit me. Lancelot! Lancelot who had 'coal-black curls hanging down'. Why did I think of that now?

'Put it away, darling. I just meant you to look.'

I slipped the photo back behind the end-piece. She handed me the picture of Billie.

'It was just a bit of a shock.'

'I'm sure I'll find him, Mother.'

shopping

Inspector Tennyson was not in. The switchboard wearily promised to relay my message 'the minute he arrives'. The newspaper lay open at the small paragraph. Evian had brought it in:

> Police believe the body found in a Surrey wood last week may be that of 36-year-old Rosetta Stirling who disappeared from . . .'

I couldn't take it in. 'Thirty-six. Same age as me.'

The phone rang. It must be Tennyson. I jumped for it before Evian could get it.

'Haydon, good. I've got you in person.' Christine. 'I'm so sick of your answering service. No, don't hang up. I know you've got my messages. You must come round.'

'I can't.' I looked down at the newspaper. Finish one job before you start another.

'Haydon, don't be an old stick. We all bleed.'

How much did she bleed when they hacked her limbs off? How had I got involved in all this? A woman who looked elegant with a shotgun?

'Haydon, it was such fun putting you to bed. You kept babbling on about never having been seduced by a suit of armour. I'd like to again. Haydon?'

I put my finger on the cut-off button and handed the receiver to Evian.

'Sorry, caller. The connection has been broken. Please try again later.'

She put the phone down. 'What was that? An obscene phone call? You went red and then white like a—'

'Nun falling downstairs?'

'That's better. Wrong punchline, but at least it's a try.'

'Evian, I feel as though I'm breaking up. Me, I used to lecture people on stress. I can see all the symptoms. I shake when I wake up in the morning. I'm drinking too much. I've stopped eating.'

'It'll all be over soon. They wouldn't say it if they weren't sure.'

'"Believe" that's what it says.'

'They can't be one hundred per cent sure because of the state it's in. But they know. It's her.'

'I didn't even know her name, Evian, her real name.'

'Yeah.'

The phone rang again. Evian answered it. Her face sagged. 'I'll tell her.'

I heard the clink of the phone going down at the other end. She held it out to me stupidly. 'Grazeley. He wants to meet you twelve o'clock tomorrow at the Silver Spur.'

'What's that?'

'Club. Straight, not sex or anything. Dining and gaming.'

'What does he want to see me for now?'

Evian shrugged, pointed to the newspaper. 'That, I suppose. Didn't you promise to drop it if it turned out to be Rusty?'

'Do you think he'll believe me?'

'Why not? There's nothing anybody can do for her now. Except find her next of kin.'

112

I couldn't fathom Evian. She had just walked into the office, dropped the paper on my desk and pointed to the page. She had said nothing about what she felt. She, who cried over broken fingernails, had not shed a tear.

'I don't think you should be afraid of Grazeley.' She said it as if she didn't care one way or the other.

I remembered my promise to Bernie. I'd been neglecting her. I brought in a jean jacket and some trousers, all miles too big for her, from my hoard. She tucked the legs into her hiking boots and professed herself well pleased. All we needed to shop for was underwear and T-shirts.

Her short legs covered a lot of ground. I had difficulty keeping up. She led me round various shops whose names were monosyllables. We ended up in But. . . She knew exactly what she wanted.

'You wait here.' She took a red check work shirt, a vest and a couple of short-sleeved sports shirts and disappeared into a cubicle.

I walked round the racks, holding things up on their hangers, examining labels. The clothes were casual, androgynous. Not quite me.

I caught sight of myself in a mirrored pillar. Did the young things riffling through the stands of cycling shorts think I was somebody's mother? My hair was still black naturally, cut in a straight bob that had been in and out of fashion for most of the century. My clothes were a little too neutral, camel slacks and cream blouse. The blouse was silk, with tiny covered buttons and a scalloped embroidered collar. One of my collection, of course.

Someone bumped me and I moved over to a wire barrel marked 'Clearance'. There were pieces of underwear in printed cotton that would barely fit a baby. I held up a cropped vest with red and black roses. Who'd wear that? A stick-insect of a girl flicked a glance at my breasts, smiled and took it out of my hand.

I moved off to graze the sports shirts. They were an atrocious price, but I could just about imagine myself wearing one. I picked a jade green one and held it up to my neck to see the effect.

It made my eyes look yellow. Kind people call them hazel. They're greeny-grey, with brown and gold flecks and a pale corona round the pupil like an eclipse. They're very deep, and the skin round the sockets is covered with a craquelure of fine lines: my eyes are the oldest part of me. In Bernie's picture they had a kind of guarded sadness, but now when I looked they were just weary. What was taking her so long?

I picked up a long-sleeved red top. Red is a very danger-ous colour for me: it has to be just the right shade. I took it over to the window. Bernie motioned to me from outside. I hung the top on the nearest hook and went after her. She nodded at me, then slid into the crowd.

I had to follow her. I'd seen the red check collar under her bomber jacket. She was half-way up the street the next time I saw her, ducking into a side turning. I ran but she was nowhere when I reached the alley.

Then I saw, across the main road, a flash of uncombed hair and dusty black nylon. I nearly collided with a taxi. The driver braked and leant on his horn. A little unnecessary I thought: the traffic wasn't going that fast. I'd lost her again.

I pulled into the wide marble doorway of a bank out of the way of the slow-moving herds of tourists. I hated central London at this time of year. April to September you couldn't move for tourists. Where was the recession? Then there was Christmas shopping and January sales. That left February and October. I must be mad to pay for an office for two months' joy a year.

Cheer up, Haydon, maybe you won't have to. You could be in prison. They pay housing benefit, I wonder if they'd pay the rent on your office. How could she, after I'd let her sleep in my office and virtually got her the keys to a flat of her own? No, Haydon, you should have known. You can't trust anybody. Grow up before you grow old.

I slumped back to the office. Of course she was there, sitting in my seat grinning in her new shirt and vest.

'Why?'

She stroked the arms of her shirt. 'It's nice, comfortable, warm.'

'You didn't have to steal it.'

'I did.' She laughed. 'Private property is theft. Anyway, d'you see the prices? Ridiculous. Robbery.'

'It's not funny, Bernie. You could have got into serious trouble.'

'They'd have to catch me first. Anyway, Holloway's full of dykes.'

I put my arm round her. Her forehead was just level with my breast. 'Please, Bernie. Promise me. No more. I know you think you're a big strong woman, but don't joke about prison. They'd cut you up in tiny little bits and eat you for breakfast. Promise?'

She looked up at me, and the adoration I saw in her eyes made my stomach churn. I pushed her away. 'Besides, I'm an accessory, knowing you've stolen those things. If I were the decent citizen I pretend to be I'd march you off back to the shop to make a full confession and pay for them.'

She rolled her eyes.

'I'm not going to. I couldn't bear the expression on the

115

police officers' faces. Just don't do it again while you're within a hundred miles of me.'

She jumped up and tried to plant a kiss on my lips but I turned and she caught the corner of my mouth. 'I love you,' she said.

'No, you don't. You just think you do. You want a mother-substitute. You'll grow out of it.'

She had that look on her face again, the one that won't be told.

the body

'Your policeman called.'

I was getting dependent on Evian. I wondered if she'd be an allowable business expense. I could trade in the answering machine. It was cheaper, but less comfort.

'Did he leave a message?'

'Something about a tea house.'

'Is that code or what? You'll never make a secretary.'

'He sounded nice. I like older men.' She twiddled a ringlet of phone wire.

'How could you tell his age over the phone?'

'He was very polite. He wasn't groping me down the line. Here.' She handed me a neat, perfectly explicit message.

The Imperial Garden Tea House was not as grand as its name suggested, but had the advantage of quiet. He stood up as I came in and extended a hand to me as if I were a man. I found myself liking him, although I didn't relish the purpose of our meeting.

'Do you like dim sum?' he asked.

'Usually. I'm feeling a bit queasy today, though.'

'We can just use them as cover. I feel a bit like a double agent coming here.'

He smiled and the stark lines of his face softened. It was a good smile, kind, asexual, what one might call paternal if it were not for the connotation.

'I do like China tea, though,' I said, consciously trying to unfreeze the muscles of my face.

'Shall I be Mother? That's another spy thing, isn't it?' I liked the way he poured, in a graceful almost balletic arc. I've noticed men have a brutal way with tea, usually.

'It's not pleasant what we've got to talk about,' he said. He settled the pot on its matching saucer. 'Do you want to ask me questions? Is that how we do it?'

I nodded but then I couldn't think what to ask. I blew on the surface of my tea. The steam fell back and made swirling oily patterns on it. 'Well, what was it like?'

A waiter came with a bamboo basket of steamed dumplings. They sat pale and puffy on their white napkin. We both looked and thought the same thought. I put my hand to my mouth.

'No.' He shook his head. 'Much worse. Have you ever bought a rabbit from the butcher and tried to imagine it running round with its fur on?'

I shook my head. 'Rabbits look too much like dead babies to me.'

'That's the point. They don't look like dead rabbits. It, she, looked terrible, a mess, but she didn't look like a dead woman.'

The dim sum steamed. They had taken on a waxy look as they cooled. Little pouches of pastry pinched together at the top. Like severed breasts. I felt the sick rising in my throat. I breathed in the steam of my tea, took a sip.

I had to ask it. I waited till my voice was steady. 'Was she . . . ? What was . . . ? I mean, what was the extent of . . . ?'

'The mutilation?'

I nodded quickly.

'The torso was untouched. There was no evidence of bruising, even, except for . . .'

118

'What?'

'The garments she was wearing had left marks. Under the skin, I think. I'm not a pathologist. It was in the reports. They were puzzled.'

'Was she wearing them when they found her?'

'No.'

'How did they identify her?'

'You speeded things up. About her being a redhead. I got on to the local lads. It solved a couple of puzzles for them.'

'But she can't have been the only missing redhead.'

'With dyed pubic hair.'

'What did you say?' Chantal said it was natural. She should know.

'Yes. It had been dyed very recently.'

'Does it really grow when you're dead?'

'Not much. It's dead anyway. The rest of the body just catches up.'

'I'm going to have to use the toilet.'

When I came back, the dumplings had been replaced by tiny spring rolls on a plate of fried seaweed.

'We'd better eat something,' he said. 'They'll think we're health inspectors.'

I nibbled a bit of seaweed. It was sweet and crunchy. I tried to put the image of the livid dyed pubis out of my mind. 'What will happen now?'

'See if anything turns up for a positive identification.'

'What do you mean? I thought you knew it was her?'

'We've a pretty fair bet. But that's not the same. It'll be an open file till we find the rest.'

The rest.

'Head and hands, that's what we rely on. That's why he did it.'

I stared at him.

'The removal of the limbs and the head. Rosetta had tattoos on her shoulder and thigh, a bluebird and a rose. It's unusual to cut them off so high up. They usually spl— I am sorry, Miss Aachen. It's a rotten job.'

'No, go on, tell me the rest of it. I've nothing left to be sick with. What do they usually do?'

'Split the bone, or saw through it. This one, the corpse was jointed.'

'How? I mean, what with?'

'Heavy cleaver probably.'

'Isn't that a clue? Can't you tell . . .'

'No. You walk through Chinatown, any supermarket, you'll see them hanging up. Have you ever seen a Chinese chef at work? Take a bird, thwack, chump, fifteen seconds and it's in eight pieces.'

'I hope that wasn't—'

'A sexist pun. No, I don't make jokes like that. And I wasn't trying to imply a Chinese villain. Crime's a very racist profession, like the law. People tend to do in their own. I wonder if there's a word for it. Like endogamy/exogamy, marrying in, marrying out. What would you call killing your own kind?'

'Murder.'

'I suppose you're right. Look, I am sorry, Miss Aachen. For all of it.' His gesture took in the table as if the dim sum were to blame. 'I don't suppose you come across a lot of death in your ordinary working life.'

'More than you'd think. Thank you, Inspector, for sparing the time. I know you didn't have to.'

'One thing, Miss Aachen.'

I was standing up. It was taking all my energy. I flopped back down. 'Yes?'

'You never asked the cause of death.'

120

'I thought . . .'

'Asphyxiation.'

My mouth opened of its own accord. Nothing came out.

'Because of the damage to the neck, post-mortem,' he said. 'We can't be more exact as to what—'

'She wasn't shot?'

'Shot? What made you think that?'

It was terrible to think of Rusty suffocated or strangled and my only feeling a lifting of pressure from my chest. A great weight off my mind, off my lungs. I never really believed it. It runs in the family. Guilt.

'Sorry. I'm confused. It's the stress of the last few days. I keep slipping in and out of an old film.'

'I know. It's shock. It gets people in funny ways. Good-bye, Miss Aachen.'

We shook hands. His were warm and dry and there were large brown spots on the pale beige skin of their backs. When I looked at them I wanted to cry, but I was all cried out.

a graze with grazeley

The Silver Spur held the kind of silence that spelled money. The deep carpets, velvet curtains, the fine table-linen cocooned the club from the street noise. Dark-suited men talked millions in low tones. Waiters and croupiers seemed to glide on cushions of air. Even the chips seemed to be padded.

In all this discretion, Grazeley's goons stood out like gilded thumbs. Nobody had told them that too much gold is almost as cheap as none. True, the suits were dark and expensively tailored. But their shoulders did not have the soft droop of business lunches, more the hard set of weighted body bags.

'Mr Grazeley is expecting me,' I said.

One examined my card. Attainment Level 1 in reading, I guessed. He'd have difficulty with 'consultant'.

The other returned a few minutes later. 'Mr Grazeley will see you now.'

I expected a sort of Donald Pleasance character: bald and sinister with glittering psychopathic eyes. He was young with the remains of a stark muscular body. Only now dissipation sat on it like soft butter – little pads of fat under his eye sockets. The neck, which had once braced and knotted like steel cable, was swaddled in excess flesh. The effect was somehow more shocking for the baby-pink cheeks and untroubled blue eyes.

'Have a seat, Miss Aachen.'

He picked up a book that lay open on the chair in front of him. He put it away in a drawer and pushed the chair towards me. I just caught the author's name on its spine but not the title. Mary Wesley. You don't get to choose your readers.

'It's all right.' He noted my barely suppressed shudder. 'You won't catch anything here. We have the place disinfected regularly.'

His upper lip didn't move when he smiled. It unnerved me.

I looked down at his shoes. Caramel-coloured glacé leather loafers, oatmeal socks and shins tanned a shade darker than the shoes. That said money, more money than the gold-hung buffoons that guarded his lair.

The blue eyes were candid. 'Maybe you don't appreciate, Miss Aachen, that your presence has an unsettling effect on my girls. All this talk about disappearances. Nobody's disappeared. These girls just come and go.'

He didn't know? Or was this a fiendish ploy? 'Didn't you get my note?'

'What note, Miss Aachen? I got your card. From several sources. And complaints. I'm a busy man. I granted you an interview to sort this business out once and for all.'

'Perhaps I can save you the trouble. I believe Rusty's been found. My search is almost over.'

'That's good news. As I said, girls come and go. It's a hazard of the industry. Now, no more talk of mysteries, unpleasantness.'

Either he was very clever or very stupid.

'Mr Grazeley, haven't your minions told you? Rusty didn't just up and leave for another town. She didn't come home. She didn't pack any bags. None of her clothes were gone—'

'I don't think you've understood, Miss Aachen.' He shook his head, reminded me of my bank manager.

'Don't you care what's happened to her?'

'I have a business to run. Mobility's just one of the many things I have to deal with. It does not help for you to go upsetting the other girls.'

'Aren't you even interested where she was found?'

'Miss Aachen, you know what they call it in our business? Not a very nice name, and it's very slippery. That is the end of it.'

'No, Mr Grazeley, not the end. Rusty's dead. I've given up the search, but you'll be hearing from the police.'

Not a blink. 'So kind of you to give me prior warning. But I don't think I'll have any trouble with the police. Now, if you'll excuse me.'

He took the book out of the drawer and started reading it as Goldfinger ushered me out.

Grazeley was so cool I would have believed him. I did believe him. Until I saw the black car ease out of the parking space at the back of the Silver Spur.

street cleaning

I'd made a pyramid of paper-clips and was just gingerly placing the last one when Evian crashed through the door. She usually moves with a studied delicacy. Now her limbs seemed to have grown several sizes larger.

'Bastards, I hate 'em. Shit, shite and shag-a-rat.' She'd lost all her finishing-school French and reverted to pure Yorkshire.

After she'd given my desk a good kicking, I asked her what had happened.

'They picked me up for soliciting when I wasn't even bloody working. I was just standing on the corner waiting for a gap in the traffic to cross the road. I can't have been there more than five seconds.'

'Really?' I found her outrage quite comical.

'Yes, bloody really! I wouldn't be so sodding barking if it weren't true. I've got to appear next Friday.'

'Can't you challenge it? Sue them for wrongful arrest, harassment.'

'Ha bloody ha. The case of Common Prostitute against the Metropolitan Police will be heard in court number three. It really is a close bet which way this one will go. The Met only have a billion solicitors and a roomful of fabricated evidence. The complainant has a string of previous convictions. It really is hard to say who will win.' She collapsed on to my swivel chair, all dangling limbs.

125

'So what are you going to do?'

'What do you think? At least they didn't hit me this time. They've got it in for me because my brother's a copper. Like I'm family. They've got their reputations to keep up. That's why they do it.'

It was one theory. I wasn't so sure. 'Do you really think so?'

'What else would it be?'

'I don't want to worry you. I saw a black car at Grazeley's club. He said he wasn't afraid of the police. I just wonder if there's a connection. You were Rusty's friend. You put me on to the case. Maybe I'm getting paranoid.' The paper-clips chose that moment to spring out and spill everywhere.

Evian jumped. 'Shite, don't tell me things like that. Let me believe they're just normal vicious bastards. What about your friendly copper? Could you get him to put in a word?'

I phoned Tennyson. I put on my £50-an-hour voice. 'Do you think it is an acceptable use of police resources to harass innocent citizens crossing the road when there's a killer on the loose?'

'Now, hold on a minute, Ms Aachen. I'm sure your friend is upset but she does have previous.'

'You know that's not admissible evidence. Besides, it's a waste of police time. If it were the public wasting your time, you'd charge them.'

'You know the Stirling case is not our baby, and your friend was arrested by uniformed officers. They wouldn't be working on that case anyway.'

I wasn't getting anywhere. I thought of another tack. 'What are you doing about my stalker?'

'Pardon?'

'Somebody's been following us in a black car. It was in the car park of Grazeley's club, the Silver Spur.'

'Make? Registration number?'

'I didn't get to see it that close to. Look, Grazeley's in this up to his ears.'

'Ms Aachen, I appreciate this death has been deeply distressing for you, but you can't go around flinging out accusations without a shred of evidence. Especially about someone like Mr Grazeley. He is not without influence.'

'You want evidence, I'll get evidence,' I declared.

'Leave that to us, Ms Aachen, it's our job. You could be putting yourself in danger. You wouldn't believe what some young ladies carry around in their handbags. Big kitchen knives. You wouldn't do anything silly like that.'

the black car

'I didn't believe in the black car,' I said.

'Why would I lie to you?'

'Evian, you have more reasons to lie than shades of nail varnish.'

She looked down at her nails thoughtfully. 'Mmm.'

We were standing under the street light in the alley outside my office. It was getting dark. That dusky violet moment just before the lamps come on. Nothing showed its true colour.

The lamp came on.

'That's our signal.'

I handed Evian the drawstring pouch. We walked to the end of the alley together. She looked round once in both directions. Then she went right and I went left.

I did believe in the black car now, though I'd only ever seen it on the edge of my vision. That made it more frightening, gave it a lurking, panther-like quality. It was a big car, but silent. I wondered if it was following me now.

I had to strain my neck to stop myself looking over my shoulder. Don't draw attention to yourself. Shoulders back. Deep breaths. I caught the lamp-post with my shoulder. I realized I'd had my eyes closed. Stupid. Don't act so suspiciously. You're just sauntering along a Soho street, busy going somewhere or nowhere. Nobody is following you.

Think of a story, that's it. Too late for window-shopping.

You're going to meet someone. You're going to meet your lover in the Crown. Don't. Not funny.

I was suddenly swept by a memory so acute, so physical, I almost stumbled in the street. I reached a hand over to the wall to steady myself. Me in a school uniform coat that peculiar shade a cross between emerald and French navy. Teal? The sleeves too long, rubbing my dry purple knuckles. They were in a ring playing a sadistic adolescent version of that children's game 'Jenny is a-weeping'. I was standing half in half out of the game. 'Stand up and choose your lover!' eight voices shrieked. Sometimes it was all right just to watch. But you never knew. They might swing round, hook you into the game and not just into the game but into the centre of the ring while they danced round and taunted you. 'We know who you love. We know who you love.' And tore up your hidden, but not well enough, photo of the maths teacher or prefect.

Don't. There are too many things in there. Better to walk these lonely streets stalked by the black car. They're not lonely. People everywhere. Don't let it get to you. You are carrying out a perfectly sensible plan. Walk. Turn here. Cross. Nothing is going to happen. Walk on.

The black car always appeared at dusk, and disappeared when you looked at it. Like the owl of Minerva. How did it go? Wisdom always comes too late and does not stay to be examined. I had seen a black car at the Silver Spur, but there was no way of knowing whether it was the same black car Evian had claimed to see on a number of occasions. It was turning into a logic problem. If all cars were black. If some cars were black. If only black cars were following us.

I'd walked a fair way along Shaftesbury Avenue to the other side of Charing Cross Road, which I regarded as alien territory. Half an hour, we'd said. I should be getting back.

At the next set of lights, I crossed and walked back on the other side of the road. It seemed less obvious than doing a U-turn in the middle of the pavement.

Evian was already there waiting for me. 'I got you a whiskey. If you're anything like me, you'll need it.'

'I never want to do that again. Whose clever idea was it anyway?'

We were giggling and hugging each other with relief. I thought of sneak visits after lights-out to smoke in toilets or to swap illicit books. It wasn't only the smoke that made you dizzy: the fear was like champagne, tingling your finger-ends and making you laugh. It was easy to forget, amid the giggles, that Evian could never have been at a girls' boarding school.

Bernie found us there, hunched together over our drinks, talking in high mad voices.

'I got the number.' She looked dusty and serious, an old woman before her time. 'It was a Sierra, I think. A big Ford anyway.'

'You think?' Evian raised her eyebrows.

'You didn't ask me for the make.' She slumped down into a chair, a compact lump like a bag of coal.

She's a very graceless child, I thought. She pulled her sleeves down over her hands, then leaned her chin on them.

'Why are you looking so miserable? Which one of us did he follow?' I asked, too sharply.

'You,' she said, indicating me. Evian pouted.

'Did you get a look at the driver?' I asked. 'Would you recognize him?'

'You're so clever. Don't you know?' she growled. Then she scraped her chair round and stomped up the stairs.

'What's up with her?' Evian asked. She shrugged and turned her attention back to her drink.

'Evian, you never bought her a drink.'

'She's too young for it.'

I didn't anticipate any problem with Tennyson. He sounded tired but friendly. 'Following you around, Miss Aachen? It's not the back of beyond, you know. Are you sure it isn't a legitimate road user?'

'Please, Inspector, you have access to the computer. It'll only take a couple of minutes. Just to set my mind at rest.'

'OK, Miss Aachen, give us the number. I'll make a few enquiries. As if I don't have enough work to do already.'

'I think it's a black Sierra.' I read out the number and asked him to read it back to me.

There was silence on the other end of the phone.

'Are you there, Inspector? Did you get the number? Can you repeat it for me?'

'Do you think I have nothing better to do with my time, Miss Aachen? I've already pushed my nose into somebody else's murder enquiry. Perhaps you'd like me to fetch your shopping afterwards.'

'Insp—'

The phone was slammed down.

'I don't know what I said.' I stared at the burring handset. 'Did I sound patronizing?'

Evian looked up from some invisible mending on her nail. 'No more than usual.'

'Thanks. I don't understand what's happening.'

'You're crying!' said Evian. 'Do you think it's a full moon? Makes people emotional.'

nicked

'What did he mean about Grazeley having friends?' I asked Evian. 'Was it a serious threat?'

'Is the Pope Catholic? Does shit stink?'

'I take it that's a yes. What could he do to me?'

'Where would you like me to start?'

'You're being very Delphic today, Evian. Seriously, what could he do to me?'

She pulled off her middle fingernail and repositioned it. Copper wasn't her colour. I said as much.

'Mmm,' she agreed. 'He could break your nails, then your fingers, then your hands, then . . .'

'If we had evidence . . .'

'Big if.'

'What do we actually know? She was due to meet Billie in her break. Several people confirm that. We don't know if she ever met him. She was due on for the second half of her act. We don't know if she ever intended to show. Did she meet Billie? Did she catch that train? We have to find him, or someone who was working with her before she went on her break. She must have told somebody of her intentions.'

'Do you think they'd talk? Maybe we're not the only ones being followed.'

My throat went dry. I had spent three days on the training file and ticked off phase one on my wall planner. I didn't

want to believe my diligence was due to Mr Grazeley's
threats. If that's what he could do to me, what chance had a
little boy? I didn't want to think about that.

'I'm not cut out for trailing round those clubs,' I said.
'Could you do some asking? She was supposed to be your
friend.'

Evian looked appalled. 'I've had enough surgery to last
me a lifetime. He'd think nothing of getting me cut up.
You're safe because you're respectable.'

Then she took my hand, which was unusual for Evian.
For someone in her profession she had an odd aversion to
physical contact. Her hand was hot and slightly damp. There
was fear in her wide black pupils. She squeezed my hand.
'Please, Haydon. For me.'

'I'll give Paradise Now one more try, see if I can recon-
struct her movements. After that, if I haven't got any further,
I give up.'

I never got to Paradise Now.

I stopped off at a chemist's for some pain-killers. The
stress was giving me headaches and my shoulders were tight
as granite. I slipped the pack into my raincoat pocket.

I stood on the corner dithering about whether to buy an
evening paper. Several people brushed up against me. I'd
taken to reading all the tiny articles tucked away at the
bottom of other columns, about crimes and strange occur-
rences. I wasn't consciously looking for more on Rusty but
I'd never been interested before.

I had just decided against: I didn't want to develop lurid
appetites. I turned away from the news-stand. A heavy hand
clapped on to my shoulder. I swung back laughing: one of
Evian's jokes. I looked up into the face of a tall dark-haired
man. My nose was level with his lapel. There was something
familiar about him.

'Haydon Aachen?' He flashed something that could have been a warrant card. 'DS Scott.'

'Yes, how can I help you?'

'If you'd like to accompany me to the station.'

'Why?' It had to be a joke.

'Unless you'd rather I searched you in the street.'

'Search? Don't be ridiculous. You can't search me.'

'Police and Criminal Evidence Act allows me to make a search in a public place if I have reasonable grounds for belief that you are carrying quantities of controlled drugs.'

'Which Section? Drugs? The only drugs I've got are . . .' I put my hand into my pocket and pulled out the packet. 'Oh, my God.'

In my hand, instead of the chemist's bag with the twenty-four foil-wrapped pain-killers, was a plastic self-seal envelope of white powder.

'Yes?'

I was jabbering. 'B-b-but. It's a plant. I've been set up. Someone . . . Grazeley!' The plastic bag now had my finger-prints all over it. People were stopping to stare at me. 'I'll go down to the station but it's a mistake.'

On the way I tried yoga breathing exercises, mantras, all the relaxation techniques I knew. They worked to an extent. My heart rate slowed to near normal. Then I worried that they'd think my serenity was chemically induced. DS Scott had slipped the powder bag into another bag and thence to his pocket. He was wearing gloves.

At the door of the police station my anxiety level rocketed. I felt it as a stabbing pain in my lower back. Up till then I hadn't really accepted that this was happening to me. I felt a whoosh of adrenaline to my legs, and it was all I could do to stop myself from making a run for it. Instead I started screaming for my lawyer. DS Scott smiled at me.

'I'm not making a statement without legal representation. I know my rights.'

DS Scott nodded at the man behind the desk. 'Any tea going?'

Calm down. This is not *Miami Vice*. Shoulders down, neck loose, drop jaw. I was once told, during an examination, that relaxing the mouth muscles relaxes the vagina. I wondered if it worked for the other bits. Breathe 1–2–3–4. Hold 1–2–3–4. Out 1–2–3–4.

He was leading me down into the bowels of the building. Some part of my mind noted that I hadn't been cautioned or charged. Maybe the police thought there was something fishy about it. It was too convenient the powder being in my pocket when I was stopped. What was it? Heroin? Cocaine? What was the brown lumpy stuff? Crack? It wasn't crack.

He led me to a room that was furnished only with a table and two chairs. I sat down and repeated that I wouldn't say anything without a solicitor. I didn't have a solicitor except for one who did the conveyancing on my flat. I could phone up a law centre and ask them to get hold of the duty solicitor. They were probably quite used to cases like this. Did they still call them drug busts or was that dated slang?

'All right,' said DS Scott. He sat down in the other chair.

He was a very attractive man. He was built like a rugby player. His hair was a touch too long for a policeman; a dark lock flopped into his left eye. It gave him a rakish dangerous look more suited to a romantic poet. Coal-black curls hanging down. Where had I read that recently? My mind was rambling.

I felt suddenly lonely. He would not know what it was like. I couldn't imagine him ever sitting alone at a table.

There would always be women flowing over him, touching him with glamour.

He smiled. His silence filled the room. It was hot. My breathing had gone 5–3–2.

'You don't really believe I was carrying drugs,' I said, to relieve the tension in my chest. It was hardly a confession. 'Who told you to pick me up? Was it an anonymous tip-off?'

He shook his head.

'It was Grazeley, wasn't it? He got someone to plant that bag on me, then phoned you.'

He raised his eyebrows. His silence was unnerving.

'It must have been Grazeley.'

'Who is Grazeley, Miss Aachen?'

'He owns lots of clubs round here. He's Mr Big in the flesh business. I wouldn't be at all surprised if he was a major drug dealer.'

DS Scott nodded. He had a curly, Celtic mouth made for witticisms. Or, some women might think, for kissing. He just said, 'Do go on.'

'Grazeley's already warned me off. I've been asking questions, you see, about one of his girls. That's what he calls them. A woman named Rusty. You said you saw her the night she disappeared.' I remembered where I'd seen him before. 'It looks like her body's turned up. Killed.'

'Oh, yes. And what have your investigations revealed?'

I couldn't tell if he was mocking me. I ploughed on anyway. 'Well, I haven't actually discovered anything yet, but I must be close because he's obviously frightened. There's a boy, also, who's disappeared.'

'A boy?'

'Yes, Wee Billie, vanished without trace. I haven't been able to get any sort of a lead on him. I think he might be a material witness.'

136

There was a tapping on the door. Scott poked his head out and there was a whispered conversation.

He came back in, smiled and sat down. 'Where were we? Yes, Mr Big and a boy.' He put his head on one side, nodding for me to continue.

'There's not much more to it. I haven't really found anything out, but somebody's very keen to stop me before I do.'

He looked down at his hands for an abnormally long time. My chest tightened.

'That is the biggest load of cobblers I've ever heard in my life. The only explanation for such a fantasy is that you're still high on whatever substance it is you sell. I'm going to have to search you.'

His snarling face was an inch from mine. I jumped up. He jumped up and kicked the chair away from me.

'Right. Stand there. Bend over. Elbows on the table.'

I stood frozen. This couldn't be right. 'You can't do this. I want a woman. You can't search me without a doctor or a policewoman.'

'I want a woman!' he mimicked. His face was red and strangulated. 'It's all right for them to get their dirty little fingers on your cunt. What did she do for you? What do you like? Bitch!'

I leaned on the table for support. My legs were gone. This couldn't be happening. Not in a police station.

'That's it. Bend over, it'll be easier if you co-operate.' He was breathing hard. There was a peculiar ritual quality to his voice, as if the form of words were important, rote.

No, I couldn't be hearing this. I closed my eyes. Images of blood danced before them. Pools of red, Rusty's net dress, the ruby, Scott's congested face, Evian's nails. Red. Red. No. I clung to the table edge. My body was soaked in warm . . . No. *No*. Breathe 1–2–3–4. The table was slipping away from me. The floor lurched.

The door swung towards me. 'Out, Scott!'

Out damned spot. That was Macbeth. Blood will have blood. The table crashed towards me. Somebody put a chair under me and I sat back, head wobbling. A woman's hands pressed a glass of water to my lips. Then she went out and shut the door behind her.

I was left alone with Tennyson. He held up the plastic bag of white powder. 'Sorry, Miss Aachen.' He threw it on the table. 'Canteen sugar. Somebody's idea of a joke.'

I blinked at him.

'You're free to go, Miss Aachen. We're not charging you.'

'He was going to . . .' What? I shook my head. It was happening again: fainting fits, delusions, the colours. I didn't know how much of it I'd imagined.

'Pardon?'

'Nothing.'

I put my head on my office desk. My forehead was damp from the bathroom. I'd been sick. Again. I seemed to spend my life being sick.

Right, think it out. Face it. Evian's black eyes swam before me. Much worse things had happened to her. Put in a men's prison. Rapes. Countless beatings.

'They can't do that, Evian. Put in a complaint. Sue them.'

Evian's eyes gummy with distress, bruised. 'Why are you so stupid, Hallie? You know why they pick on me especially, because of my brother. They hate it, you know, when there's a copper in the family, like it reflects on them.'

Well, that was me done for, then. Besides, where was the

evidence? Assault did not require physical harm. Just that the victim should be put in fear. But without a mark on my body, it was my word against his. Forget it, H. Next time it will be heroin.

water

The police had already told Chantal. I felt I still had some duty to perform in respect to her. I had a nagging feeling there was something she could tell me about the night Rusty disappeared. She knew Billie, maybe she knew where he would go.

Someone, possibly at the instigation of the police, had cleaned up. I wasn't doubled up with the smell as I had been on my previous visit.

Chantal looked worse, though. She was wearing a housecoat that had been peach. It had an edging of finely worked lace, grey now. It matched her skin. The housecoat drooped open: it was much too big for her. Her breasts showed like a pair of gaunt eyes in shadowed sockets.

She didn't say anything as she led the way in, as if it were a job she was trained to, showing people in, sitting down and staring. As if she did it several times a day.

'I'm sorry, Chantal.'

She nodded, as if that, too, were a job.

'It's a terrible thing.'

Nod.

'What will you do now?'

'Go back to work I suppose.'

I bit my lip. All the objections I wanted to raise would sound cruel or crude.

She laughed. More like a hum, really. 'You think no one

would have me. In this state. You don't know nothing, love. Some men'd fuck anything. I was going to say if it moved. They don't even care about that. Cold cunt, they call it. Sounds like a buffet. Do you think he did that to her?'

'I don't know, Chantal. Didn't the police say?'

'Big words, I don't know what the fuck they said. There was one. Big bloke. I could tell. You know, the questions he was asking.'

'You could tell what?'

'That he was going home to wank over it.'

My stomach did a backward flip. There didn't seem to be enough air in the room.

'That shock you? It don't me. I seen 'em all, punters. Plenty of perverts in uniform too. You know the number: give it to us or we'll pull you. I said I'd rather fucking go to jail. Pity she didn't, eh? Think he did that to her?'

'Who? What?'

'Don't matter. I'm rambling. Their fucking questions. What difference does it make? Suppose you want to know, and all?'

'Chantal, all I came round for was to say I'm sorry about Rusty and to see if there was anything I could do.'

'It's a nice name, innit? If I'd a known, I'd of called her Rosie more often. That's what she had on her shoulder. Just here. Red it was.'

She pulled open the housecoat and pointed to a spot directly above her armpit. Her skin was a grey-beige and under it, across her breasts, ran fat blue rivers of veins. The breasts seemed to collapse on to the grey bars of ribs below. She saw me looking and smiled.

'She had the most beautiful tits. I'd lie there for hours sucking them. She used to say: wash that shit stink off you and come and have yourself a bit of the real thing. She was funny, Rosie. Don't seem worth it, washing, now. What for? Punters don't give a fuck, they'd stick it into anything. She was really clean, always in the bathroom.'

I thought of Rusty dyeing her hair in secret. All of it. I caught on to the only hook she had given me. 'Chantal, you must bath. Not for them. For yourself. For her.'

She lifted her hands and then let them drop as if the weight were too much.

'Come on. I'll run it for you.'

I didn't know what sort of heating she had. I was surprised the services were still connected. I found a switch for her immersion heater. Half an hour to heat up.

The bathroom wasn't especially filthy, but I scrubbed and scoured till the tiles shone. I even polished the taps. I didn't delude myself that this was anything other than avoidance tactics. There was too much nakedness in that room. I'd felt the pinch of guilt when I looked at her breasts, as if my admiration of them on another occasion had caused all this. I knew it didn't make sense. I knew what I was trying to rub out with the gritty white cream cleaner. But she did end up with a clean bathroom.

I emptied half a bottle of Body Shop bathing bubbles into the bath.

'Chantal, come on. It's ready.'

She dragged across to the door, then stood transfixed by the steam.

'Raspberry. Oh, Rosie!'

The tears seemed to come from nowhere. Like a shower head that's barely on, they welled in a round and fell in fat dribbles. 'Rosie-eee.'

I took her skinny arm and pushed her towards the water. Her robe fell off her and she perched on the side, her buttocks sharp and blue from the pressure.

I gave her twenty minutes to soak, then came in to check. The mountain of bubbles had subsided to a thin skim. There was still a faint scent of raspberry but mingled with something I associated with sickbeds.

'You'll have to wash your hair. Do you want me to?'

It didn't look any different wet; it must have been rank. I found a plastic measuring jug on the side, filled it from the bath. Her skin had the bluish transparency of skimmed milk. Water ran down it like rain on glass. I filled my hand with a thick opal swirl of shampoo. I massaged her skull like a baby's.

She lay back on my hands and closed her eyes. I could see a faint blue marbling of veins on her lids. Even, after all this, her bones were something to take your breath away. I thought of Donatello's *Death of the Virgin*. How apt!

I filled the jug with clean water, and rinsed. The swirl of bubbles broke into the whiter foam of the bath, like cream into egg white. When at last her hair hung black and squeaky I went to fetch a towel. It should have been thick and blue and soft, but there was none of that. In the end, I brought her a clean sheet from the airing cupboard and a tea towel for her hair.

She dressed and made me tea.

'You're funny, int you? When you first came round I hated you. Just like that bitch that took my baby away. It was the skirt that done it. Can't always tell, can you?'

'No.'

'I know you done your best to find Rosie – Rusty. It weren't your fault.'

We stood clumsily at the top of her stairs, waiting for a closing gesture.

'Get on,' she said. 'I can't very well kiss a social worker.' She slapped me on the back. Like a feather.

'Find the boy. That's what she'd a wanted. You can keep the ring. I'm not going to need it where I'm going.'

I look down. My stomach slips its moorings. The drop goes on for ever. The rushing water.

'Goodbye.'

antique silk

'At least explain to me in person.'

Christine wore me down. Now I knew the cause of death, I had to see her out of politeness. I couldn't really imagine her strangling Rusty in a fit of jealousy. She wasn't like any wronged wife I'd ever come across. My suspicion was more panic on my own behalf.

I agreed to see her. 'There is unfinished business between us,' I said, trying for a cool professional tone.

'I'll say, you vixen,' she gurgled.

'No. I didn't mean . . . Hell!'

'Supper. Something light. And we'll go easy on the alcohol, given your susceptibility.'

I opened my mouth to explain. Then I thought it would be better done in person as she'd said. I found myself agreeing to supper. I'd intended a businesslike meeting on neutral ground.

She's not dangerous, I kept telling myself, so why do I feel I've taken the first step into a trap?

Bernie sulked for the rest of the day. I finally confronted her in the ladies', where she was washing her face.

'I didn't know you could whistle,' she wailed, and ran out. I wasn't even aware that I had been.

Evian called round for her early-evening fingering of my possessions. She liked to leave a hint of her perfume on everything and her gold cigarette tips in my ashtray just to remind me of her proprietorial rights.

'Poor mite's jealous,' she diagnosed. 'I do think you're awfully cruel, Belle Dame Sans Merci, taking her in as your lapdog then going to play footsie with the lioness.'

'Lioness is it?'

'*Bien sûr*. Anyway, I thought you were tangling with hubby.'

'I don't want to tangle with anybody. Not sheet-wise. I'm just intrigued by the pair of them, their relationship.'

'Well, the munchkin will be pleased there's nothing in it. Curious,' she murmured, turning my chin to catch the light, 'I never noticed before you had such high colour in your cheeks.'

'Shut up, Evian. I told you I'm not interested.'

Evian didn't say anything, just wagged a carmine finger and licked her lips.

'Out!'

I snagged my tights on the corner of someone's luggage on the escalator between the tube and the mainline station. I could buy another pair in the shopping concourse.

I didn't have much time but I found myself paralysed to make a decision. I stood on one foot, weighing the relative merits of '7 denier look ultra sheer for that special occasion' and '15 denier with Lycra for a perfect long-lasting fit'.

'What will they come up with next?'

The voice, the unfunny laugh, scalded me with panic. Scott. He was standing barely three yards from me. There was another man with him, younger, fair-haired. They both stood sideways on to me. Between them hung a red satin lace-panelled body stocking trimmed with crimson ostrich feathers.

They weren't looking at me, hadn't seen me. My mind

was three steps behind my feet. I didn't decide. I was out, away, standing at the end of platform 17 before I'd even thought. There were two pairs of tights in my hand, unpaid for, but I wasn't going back.

He lived in Epsom, I remembered. I was glad it was a non-stopper.

The train journey wasn't so bad this time. It was later and I had a window seat. I was more scared, though. I kept catching sight of my reflection in tunnels and high-walled embankments. My eyes were too bright, feverish, like a child before a party. It would end in tears.

My mother had washed and pressed the black and white tea dress and returned it by van. I wore it for luck. And a black Mexican necklace of painted stones. I never wore jewellery. It was a stranger I saw in the dark window.

The same car picked me up. They must have had a contract with the Deerharts. I looked out this time for road signs and landmarks, but I was none the wiser when the driver eased the car backwards through the gates into the stone yard.

'Treacherous,' he said, then something about turning circles.

I looked around for a black car, not particularly hopeful. We knew the driver was male, but somehow Deerhart didn't fit.

The house was double-fronted. It had been painted recently. The windows shone white under the porch lights; the rooms behind were unlit. She stood at the top of the five stone steps as if she were part of the architecture. In the cold light, her arms glowed, the pale biscuit of unpainted stoneware.

She came down to greet me. She was solid enough. But I had a momentary illusion that she was clothed in falling

147

water. She caught my arms and the warmth was a shock. Her lips breezed my cheek.

'Haydon.'

Her eyes raised a trail of goose bumps wherever they lighted. I smiled; the muscles seemed stiff with disuse.

She led me by the tips of my fingers round the back of the house. The globes spilled light on to the garden, created pools of frosted plants.

The light in the lounge was warmer. She resolved into flesh. The dress was extraordinary. Magical. Frightening.

'I took your point about the suit of armour. I think you'll find this a little softer.' She ran the tips of her thumbs down her breasts, over her nipples, and caught a handful of the fabric from mid-thigh. 'Feel.'

My hand was shaking so much I didn't dare.

'Later then. Guess.'

It felt like a test. 'It's antique, Chinese, ' I said. 'It has the sheen of panne velvet, but no nap. Is the moiré effect in the dyeing or the weave? No, it's in the twist of the thread.'

She laughed. The tip of her tongue wet her top lip. 'Where do you get it all, Haydon?'

'My mother planned for me to be a lady. When we had a sudden drop in our fortunes, she decided I'd have to bluff my way through. She's a real catalogue of abstruse knowledge. I'm just the cheap hand-out.'

'It's all bluff, Haydon. Haven't you realized that?' She waved her arm to encompass the room. Blue, purple, silver shivered across the surface of the dress.

'No, not all. That dress cost a fortune. It's real. I'm terrified it'll rip.' The truth was I was just terrified.

'I'll step out of it before the rough stuff starts.' Her eyes seemed to sprinkle green sparks on the dress. 'Oh dear, you're not going to faint on me again?'

She led me to the table and pulled out a chair. My arm brushed against her hip. The trembling was threatening to take over my whole body.

'Water.'

The glass chinked against my teeth. I managed to get it down.

Supper was an ordeal I got through by not looking up from my plate, and answering Christine's gentle chatter with monosyllables. A tiny, silent, dark woman glided in and out with plates. Filipina, I thought, but she could have been anything. I didn't realize but I was frightened of her, too. She disappeared at a nod from Christine, after bringing in two trays, of cheese and fruit. They seemed vast for her tiny arms.

'All right, Haydon, you can relax now. You haven't said a word all evening. Would you like some fruit?'

I shook my head. It was all too lush: sunset-coloured, plump, tropical fruit and luminous star-shaped carambola. 'I'll just have a dry biscuit.'

She pulled her chair round next to mine, and reached for a nectarine. She held it out to me, glossy scarlet and orange with a comet's tail of purple. She turned it round in her pale square hand.

I wouldn't be tempted. 'Honest. Cheese and biscuits will do me.'

She put it back and took a mango, holding it in both hands, her thumbs pressed to the stem end. She closed her eyes to smell. 'Please. I can't eat it all on my own. It's too much.'

She must have taken my blink for a yes. She reached across for her knife and plate, and made fan-like slices in the top half of the mango. Yellow juice bled from the cuts.

'Am I still a suspect? Is that it?' Her green eyes washed across me, leaving me sweating.

149

'Not really. It's not a woman's crime.'

'Oh, I can be quite masculine when I want to be. I'm not used to being turned down, Haydon.'

The look she gave me then made me waver. It was not the spoiled little rich girl look I expected, it was hot and predatory. The lioness, Evian had called her. Sorceress more like. Had she tried her spells on Rusty?

'It's a new sensation, Haydon. I never knew that being refused could be so erotic. The more you shiver and primp and play the nun, the wilder I get. Is that male enough for you?'

She lowered her eyes to the fruit, tugged to free a slice. It wouldn't come.

'I can't,' I said.

She pulled it free. Little peaks of orange flesh clung to the fibres of the stone. She offered the crescent to me. I took a small bite.

'Not like that. Properly.' She pulled off another slice roughly, sank her teeth into it, then sheared them along the tough red skin to catch the last of the sweet-perfumed pulp. Juice dribbled down the side of her mouth. She flicked her tongue out to catch it.

I put my fruit to my mouth. It was too soft and sweet and the scent made me dizzy.

She put the side of her finger to my lower lip to stop a trail of sweet mush. I licked it, then turned my face away.

'What is it, Haydon? Is it some kind of game? See how far you can push me?'

'I'm scared,' I said. 'Of all this.'

'Ah, Cinderella!' She was very close to me now. 'Tell me about the drastic reverse in your fortune. Someone died?'

'Yes. No, it wasn't like that. I was being melodramatic. Runs in the family. We weren't really rich or anything. My mother . . .'

150

'Ummm?'

'There were about four terrible years. I just remember that period as an absence. Of everything. All the nice things disappeared overnight. I remember Mother packing away all the beautiful china and glasses in tissue paper. We drank out of mugs after that. It was as if it was some kind of punishment.'

'Who was being punished?'

'I don't know. Me. Her. His memory perhaps. The worst thing is I've seen them, the cups. It wasn't as if she'd sold them. I don't know when she took them out of their tissue paper. Why am I telling you this? You're not interested in my family history.'

'On the contrary, I'm intrigued. I want to know what made you. There is something of iron inside you. I want to know how it got there. For the last five minutes, I have been fondling your nipple. I want to know how you do that, talk tea sets.'

The bit of my mind that concerned itself with that kind of thing had, of course, been aware. It lay back like a cat, only pretending to be asleep. 'I don't know what to say.'

'You could say "Stop" or "Go on". Tell me about the deprivation. Were you ever hungry?'

'No, not in that way. It was just as if the light had gone out.'

She continued to circle my nipple with her index finger. I had to watch now. She scrolled down to my navel then back up to the other breast.

'What was the punishment for?' Her green eyes looked directly into mine.

I squirmed. 'I can't talk about it. You tell me about yourself. How come all this?' I gestured to the room, brushing her hand away as I did so. It fell on to my lap.

'I have a rich husband.'

It seemed indecent to talk about her husband while she was starting to unbutton my dress. 'How could you?'

She felt the shudder go through me. She stopped. 'Haydon, you're a prude.' Just the tip of her finger stroked the small silk-covered button. 'These are nice, so virginal, like a Victorian governess.' A pink slip of tongue showed between her teeth on the 'ess'.

I thought: I can manage anything, so long as she doesn't try to kiss me.

'Shall I tell you about my husband? The ideal husband. He doesn't, as they say in working classes, trouble me much. That was one of the attractions. He can't, you see, except under very special conditions.'

She looked at me hard. I clenched my thighs together. I thought of her soft pink husband, like Playdoh in her hands. 'Christine, I think your husband's in love with me.'

She smiled. 'That's one of them. Do you want to know the others?'

I shook my head. You didn't need to be the great detective to put John Deerhart and Christine and Rusty's tackroom gear together and work out the nature of his sexual deviation.

John Deerhart, I was sure, was incapable of deliberate hurt but . . . The ghost of an idea walked over me. Asphyxia.

'Haydon, are you all right? You went completely white.'

She was leaning over me, tapping my cheeks and unbuttoning my neck fast. The cat stretched, opened one eye, and curled back to its false sleep.

'Haydon, you're a frightening person to have around. Do you want to go to bed?'

I never know how these decisions are made. Somewhere, the mind, the brain, behind locked doors, a minute shift and everything is different. One second I was faint with fear, a mad unthinkable suspicion. The next, my desire had won. It could mess up my life to give in to it, but I couldn't repress it any longer: it would rip me apart.

I reached for her hand. 'I do want to go to bed. In a bit. You still haven't told me anything about you.'

Something passed over her face, fleeting, like a gust on water. I couldn't tell if it was pain or disappointment.

When she spoke, it was softer, as if the fight had gone out of her voice. 'What's to tell? I'm no mystery. All my appetites are healthy. I don't have any hidden depths. All my friends are in therapy. I'm not. They're married to their neuroses. I get to fuck all these gorgeous women, and they run off to their shrinks. Which would you rather?'

It had the air of a prepared speech, a little performance she put on for all her women. I didn't care. I felt on the brink of a breakthrough in the Rusty case. I didn't care. Nothing mattered. I was under her spell.

I said, 'I think all sex is a kind of psychosis.'

'It is, the way you kiss.' Her eyes were shockingly open.

Her lips. I hesitated, turned away to breathe. 'Wait.' Too much.

She was speaking again. 'You don't think I'd have gone to all this trouble if I didn't have an idea. You're like one of those dams – all that power held back. Only you can control it. I did think . . .'

I had stopped breathing. I could hear the whisper of her dress. All that weight of water. Such a long way to fall.

She turned me round to face her. 'You have to do it, Haydon. I can't force you. Not now.'

Do, do, do, my body was yelling. Make me. It was crumbling but I couldn't move. That was my problem.

dead

'The munchkin's back,' Evian informed me.

'How did she know?'

'Telepathy, *chérie*. Don't you know, when one is in love, one can feel the beloved's innermost thoughts. It is a silken thread which binds two hearts as one.'

'I hope not. I don't feel very proud of myself at the moment.'

'Oh, you heart-breaker. Across the land they fall to your fatal charm.'

'Why do they go together so, sex and death?'

'Come off it, Hallie. You're starting to believe your own publicity. Well, a girl's got to do what a girl's got to do.' She wiggled off.

That's a dead giveaway, I thought. The male and the female pelvic girdles are different. The wobbly high heels almost disguised it. A woman of Evian's build wouldn't wiggle. It was a caricature, a stylized rendition of femininity, and I resented it.

You're very touchy about femininity this morning, H. Could it have anything to do with what happened or didn't happen last night?

Because I felt changed, I expected it to show. Evian had enquired if I'd got 'the leg over'. When I shook my head, she believed me. She hadn't seen a *je ne sais quoi* radiate from me. It was all in my head.

Work was the only cure. I tipped out the drawerful of receipts on to my desk. Date, sort, enter. I must get my first VAT return in on time. I didn't want to get a bad name with the Exciseman. Where had I put my bank statements?

I spent the morning making neat, chronologically ordered piles of paper. It was then I realized that I hadn't a clue how to fill in the forms. I needed an accountant. The only one I knew was John Deerhart.

I played the conversation in my mind. Yes, Mr Deerhart, I know you think you're in love with me, but I'm in love with your wife, will you do my VAT returns? Perhaps we can have another triangle. Two triangles. More of a pentangle. Christine and me and you and Rusty and Chantal. Pentangles are powerful magic. Like rubies. Rusty's dead.

'Chantal's dead.'

'Evi—' I was going to say something about the papers on my desk. 'Did I hear you?'

'Chantal's dead. I just heard.'

The pile of papers she'd knocked over as she came in slid one by one to the floor. They went so slowly, with a little lift as they parted from the pile. It seemed like hours that I watched them fall, leaf by leaf. 'Chantal dead.'

It wasn't a joke. It wouldn't be. Evian's face was a mess of run mascara and blotches.

'There's some tissues in the drawer,' I said.

'Thanks.'

Something bad was happening in the world. Rusty. Chantal. Who next?

'What?' Evian's voice came out of a tissue.

'I said: who next?'

'Hallie, that's creepy.'

'I was going to give her the ruby.'

Evian's eyes flicked over to the wall safe. She looked horrified and, I think, guilty.

'Do you believe in bad luck, Evian?'

She nodded.

'Do you think it's like a disease that you pass on person to person?'

She was too noisy. I wanted to be alone with my thoughts. 'Come back later, Evian. I can't think.'

When she was gone I took the remains of the whiskey out of the safe, but I didn't pour it. The ruby was still in there in its blue bag. I spilled it out on to my palm. It wasn't hot. Funny, I expected it to be hot, to burn with supernatural power. That was a stupid thing to think.

It was odd. I didn't feel like crying. I didn't feel sad. I just wanted some quiet. Evian seemed to have left her grief behind her in the office, a subdued howling that rolled round and round the walls. Could people do that?

I thought of Chantal dressed in foam like a bridal gown. Would they be together? Was she already dead when I put her in the bath and washed her hair? They do that to dead people, yes. They couldn't do that for Rusty. Her fine head of red hair that wasn't red and wasn't there. What if they cut Chantal up too? Poor Chantal and her arms so thin already.

I picked up the papers and put them back on their pile. I sorted them into smaller piles. Then I put them away in new cardboard file boxes and I labelled them on the front in red felt-tip. I took all the old boxes off the shelf and dusted it and rearranged them to make room for the new. Then I cleaned the keys of my typewriter and reorganized my drawers, so all the paper-clips were with paper-clips and the rubber bands were separate. I lined up the little bottles of correcting fluid. There was a black one and several white ones and a green-labelled one that was the solvent you dilute it with.

And all the time I didn't cry.

I remembered my mother wrapping gold-rimmed cups in tissue paper and filling each with crumpled balls of the same. Chantal's hair trailing in the water like the black weed that clings to the legs of the pier. We were on holiday, just the two of us, because he couldn't get the time off. A very important case. 'It matters to me,' he shouted. He never shouted usually. Then the boy was dead. And the train. My mother packed up the sunshine and put away the seaside. That's what happens when someone dies.

I didn't cry once.

When Evian came back her eyes were heavy. My office sparkled.

'I'm distraught,' she said. I was glad she didn't say it in French. 'I've been talking to some people. Do you want the story?'

'Who killed her?'

She looked surprised in a tired sort of way. 'You can't say, can you? Her heart stopped, that's what'll be on the death certificate. If she's lucky.'

'Lucky?'

'Yeah. She was injecting something that she shouldn't. Did you know she was going back to work?'

'Oh no! Was it an overdose?'

'Not exactly. Methadone pessaries.'

'Pessaries? I don't understand. You can't inject—'

'She was desperate. She took it really badly about Rusty. She had to get back to work. She had to eat. You know what it's like.'

'But pessaries. How could she . . . ?'

157

'Don't ask. Anyway, she was in too much of a hurry. Didn't melt it properly.'

'And it stopped her heart? I'm not surprised. How horrible.'

'Hallie, you don't know what it does to me, my two best friends dying.'

I felt a tarantula crawl up my spine. H., you've got a foul mind. 'I know it must be horrible. If there's anything—'

'There is, actually.'

I'm not hearing this. It's a misunderstanding. 'Yes?'

'There is something you can do for me. I'm beside myself. I need something . . .'

I looked at her. She wasn't pretending. 'Evian, I hope you're not saying what I think you are.'

'Just twenty quid.'

'Just twenty quid,' I repeated.

'Yes. You don't know what it's like, Hallie.'

'Tell me.'

'Just to get me through the worst bit. Hallie, she was my best friend. It'd be a loan. I'd pay you back.'

'Let me get this clear in my mind, Evian. Stop me if I get it wrong. Your best friend, distraught at the death of her lover, injects herself with something that should not be injected. As a result she is dead. You, distraught at her death, want me to lend you twenty pounds, so that you can in turn inject yourself and forget your grief. Does that about sum it up?'

'You don't understand.'

'You're right there.'

'I wouldn't be stupid. I wouldn't use bad stuff. Hallie, don't be like that.'

'One question.'

'Yes?' A little light came on. She knew she'd won.

'Why twenty pounds? That won't last you long. Did you calculate how much I carry around in my purse? Did you reckon that if you said fifty I'd throw you out without a word?'

She couldn't quite hide the triumph. 'No, I worked out twenty was what I needed.'

'How much will that get you?'

She gave a sly smile. 'There are ways of making it go further.'

'Evian!'

'No, I don't mean the gear. The money. Didn't you do economics? Keynes, the multiplier.'

That was it for me. 'If you know so much about economics, how come you're working the streets, Steven?'

'You fucking bitch.'

She wouldn't refuse my money, though.

the munchkin

'I've got something for you.' Bernie's arms were facing the wrong way out and she rubbed the toe of her brown boot against the back of her jeans. This was going to be embarrassing.

'I hope you haven't been spending money.' It was a foolish thing to say. I cringed as I said it.

She held it out to me. It was in a thin white paper bag, the kind newsagents put cards or sweets into. I slipped it out carefully, trying to control my facial muscles by will.

'Oh. Really. Hey, did you do this?'

She hunched her face down into the collar of her jacket.

'Bernie, it's really good. You should go to art school. Thank you. I thought I was going to have to pretend to like it. It's really lovely.'

It was a drawing in coloured pencil of a blue vase of tulips, violas, pansies and dark pink petunias. A velvety coolness breezed off the page.

'It's incredibly good. You don't mind if I put it in another frame? I've got one at home that would go beautifully with the blue.'

'I just put it in that to stop it getting damaged. It's because you got me the interview for the flat.'

I'd forgotten to ask her how it went. 'It was only a couple of phone calls, Bernie. You must have spent ages on the picture. It went all right, then?'

She beamed. 'Be ready in a few weeks. I'm going in a hostel till then. Got a few things to sort out first. Can I make you some tea?'

'No, let's go out. Celebrate. I'll buy some cream cakes.'

'I'd rather sit in your office.' She had it bad. 'I'd like an office like this one day.' She touched my desk as if it were an altar.

'Well, you'll have to work hard and lead a blameless life.'

She nodded. I wondered when the sense of irony developed. Was it alongside wisdom teeth?

'Can I ask you something?' She picked a red paper-clip from a shoal in my desk tidy.

Here it comes. 'Ask away, Bernie.'

'That woman. Your friend said . . .'

Watch the paper-clip. Here we go, one arm straight. Now for the curved bit. 'What did my friend say?'

'That you didn't, you know, ever.'

'She would know, would she?'

The body of the paper-clip was wrenched into a buckled straightness. 'I asked her. I'm sorry. I just . . .'

'You just wanted to know whether I slept with Christine Deerhart. You, an eighteen-year-old, off the street, just waltz into my office and question me about my sexual activities. Don't you think that's a trifle impertinent? If you want an office like this, you're going the wrong way about it, my girl.'

Her face was red and wet and crumpled like a baby's. Go on, kick her again. Then maybe you'll feel better about yourself.

'Bernie, thank you for the picture. I do want us to be friends. But no more questions like that, OK?'

She nodded. Then she took a deep breath and I could see

her flexing herself to ask another question. 'It's just that . . .
I had another reason for asking.'

I put on my severest frown.

'Are you still . . . on the case? Are you looking . . . ? I
need to know.'

'Are you talking about Rusty? You know the body's been
identified, as near positive as they can be. My part of the
job's done. She's been found.'

'Yeah but—'

'But nothing. It's a job for the police.'

'You said—'

'I said a lot of things I regret. Bernie, try to look at things
logically. There's nothing I can do that the police can't do
better. While she was only missing, they could shrug it off:
Girls, they come, they go. Now they've got a dead body.
Even the most cynical policeman can't ignore that. I'm not
equipped to hunt a killer. Besides, nobody's hired me to.'

Arguments seethed across her face. Eventually she
acceded by a change of subject. 'Are you going to the
funeral?'

'Yes. Chantal's family, what there is of it, live in Deptford.
Do you want to come with me?'

'I'd like that. I wish I could send something.'

'I gave Evian twenty pounds towards a wreath.'

Her mouth flopped open.

'I said I wanted to see the receipts. I suppose it was a sort
of test.'

She just kept looking at me, shocked.

'That's another reason I'm not cut out for it. They're too
busy destroying themselves. Life's too cheap round here for
avenging angels.'

She shook her head.

162

'It's a waste,' I said. 'I think she was the most beautiful woman I ever set eyes on.'

Bernie opened her mouth and closed it again.

'Chantal. Despite everything she did to herself and what other people did, she had that kind of face. Like old film stars who still have those bones underneath the wrinkles and the falling hair.'

She was trying to keep her face grave, as befitted the subject, but relief danced like a troubled reflection on a dark pool: the most beautiful woman in the world was dead.

'Don't, Bernie. It doesn't work like that. When you get to be very old like me, you'll realize. One doesn't always desire the most beautiful, or avoid the ugly. The world isn't such a regular place as that.'

My eyes were burning. It struck me that I couldn't remember Christine Deerhart's face. Only an impression of green and silver, and the touch of a dress so soft it squeezed all the breath from my body.

'Now I think all the beautiful has gone out of the world.'

I leaned my eyes on the heels of my hands. I heard the whisper of tissue. Unseen hands were packing it all away. Sunshine. Pale porcelain. Chantal.

'Come on. Let's get some coffee.'

It was a long time and not a long time later that Bernie again brought up the subject of finding Rusty's killer. It was writhing away inside her all the time.

'I don't understand,' she said. 'What's changed? You seemed so set.'

What's changed? Couldn't she see?

'Bernie, I tried on the role of great detective and it didn't fit. I'm too vulnerable.'

I could tell by the set of her chin she wouldn't listen, she wouldn't believe me. She would cling to her image of me as strong and, in a certain way, glamorous.

I continued, anyway. 'All my normal defences, the things all of us have to protect ourselves, I've had to drop them, turn them inside out. Bernie, it's hurting me.'

She just looked that wilful look.

'I loved someone once. Not physically, you understand. We used to talk. For hours and hours. I'd hold her hand and it felt like we had the most perfect understanding. Nothing could . . . She had me locked up. In an institution. You know what that's like. Where they injected me to keep me quiet. That's why I can't go on with this. I never want to go back there.'

I thought: I've never said that to anyone. I thought I'd die rather than say it. And that tuppenny ha'penny bit just looks at me as if it's all one more great-detective pose. 'You want an angel of fire, all grand and righteous, flushing out the evil-doers, protecting the weak; it's not me. I am weak. What would I do if I found the killer?'

'Bring him to justice.'

'What does that mean? The police are still looking for the rest of Rusty's body. He's not going to confess. What sort of a case would that make? It would never get to court.'

'You could make sure he never does it again.'

'Oh, yes, a shoot-out at dawn? I don't think he's going to do it again. I don't think he meant to kill Rusty.'

She gaped in admiration. All my lectures undone. 'How do you know that?'

'Well, I have been doing some detective thinking. It was something the police said about the body. It was disposed of quite thoroughly. It was only luck it was found so soon. And he'd still made sure there were no obvious distinguishing marks, like the tattoos. So he's very efficient, quick-thinking.

'Even so, it has the look of something done in haste, covering up an error. If it was premeditated, I don't think he would have chosen Rusty. She was too distinctive. All that red hair, even if he didn't know about the tattoos. He didn't go out to kill Rusty. Maybe an accident.'

'An accident?'

'Rusty sold a particular sort of sexual fantasy. It's danger-ous stuff. She died of asphyxia. I can see how it could have been an accident. Or she may have resisted, and he restrained her with her tackle and that killed her. That would probably be manslaughter.'

'If it was an accident—'

'Why didn't he report it? He may have had some position to keep up. It might be hard to explain. She was wearing some sort of harness when she died. A businessman, for instance.'

She clapped her hand over her mouth.

'Yes, I did suspect John Deerhart. I think he played peculiar games with her. That's how the accident idea first came to me. But I'm not sure he could do that to her body.'

'He's too weak?'

'Whoever did it had to think of Rusty as just a body before she died. John Deerhart knew different. She wasn't just a body to him, not if I read him right.'

'You keep saying him. What about a strong woman?'

'Ah, the feminist defence. I thought maybe Christine Deerhart had helped him or committed the crime herself. That was before I spoke to Tennyson. I can't see her doing that to a woman's body. Christine's a bad, bad girl but not in that way. Besides, her aesthetic sense is too highly developed.'

Bernie frowned.

'Don't ask me to go into details.' I leered. That was to pay her back for her earlier impudence.

'So he gets away with it, the real killer?'

'I don't see what else I can do.'

'What if there's a witness?' she asked.

'The boy.' All roads lead back to the boy. 'But it's not the same boy.'

'What?'

'I mean, it won't happen again. He's hidden himself so well, I couldn't find him even with you helping. He's safe.'

'Not if they find him first.'

'How can they?' The photo. The black car. Some people are better at it than me. Some people have connections. 'Bernie, I need to know something. It won't get you into any trouble. Before that night that I found you in this office, had you ever been in here before?'

'No, I followed you home. You know that. But I'd never been inside here.'

'Someone broke into this office and stole the photo of Billie.'

She digested this information for a moment.

'Was it really true about you being in an institution? You weren't just saying it?'

'It's true enough. I wouldn't make it up, I assure you. But what's it got to do with anything?'

'I think I know where he is.'

'At the seaside?'

'Yeah. We better get to him first.'

Why did it feel as though it was all preordained? Like a Greek tragedy. Like Oedipus.

seaworth

I told Bernie that Billie was probably safer not being found. Even as I said it, I could feel the words dropping out of my mouth like wet pebbles. Of course I was going to go. It was written in the sand nearly thirty years ago.

Bernie thought she saw the black car. I'd started to interpret such sightings as hysterical symptoms, like poltergeists or visions of the Blessed Virgin.

We took elaborate precautions against being followed. It was fun, though, seeing most of the South of England from a train window. I felt like someone in a poem.

'What's he look like, Grazeley?' she asked.

'Young, expensive clothes, he would have been handsome a couple of years ago. He looks like he went to seed very quickly.'

'The man in the black car's handsome. Big, curly hair nearly touching the roof.'

'Big shoulders? Like they don't belong in a suit?'

Bernie nodded.

'Sounds like one of Grazeley's goons.'

Bernie explained how she suddenly came to remember the address.

'He used to send her a card, see, at Christmas and on her birthday. He got me to write it for him. He wasn't very good at writing.'

167

'I'm not surprised. He's hardly been to school in the last ten years.'

'It was her birthday last week. When it came around, I had a funny feeling. You know, you've forgotten something. It kept nagging at me. Then it came to me in a dream. I saw Wee Billie at the seaside and the address just came to me.'

It was that bit of her story I questioned. I know Coleridge was supposed to have seen the whole of 'Kubla Khan' in a dream but I'd never seen it work for us mortals. My theory was that she'd always known the address but was waiting for some sign from me that I was trustworthy. So perhaps it was worth revealing my vulnerability.

The little local train pulled into the station.

'This is it.'

I had hoped to buy a map or guide so we wouldn't have to ask the way. There were no kiosks. The ticket window was shut. A man in an ancient rail uniform was talking to a brown-legged cyclist with a back pack. I waited while he directed the man to the South Downs Way. It seemed a long ride.

'And what can I do for you, young ladies?'

'Seaview Gardens?'

'Sea. View. Gardens. Ah!' He laughed. 'That's a laugh that is. You got good eyesight? Seaview Gardens. Other side of the dock. Along the front till you come to the Anchor Café. Then you know you've come too far. So go back on yourself to a big white pub on the corner. Got an unusual name, can't rightly remember it, though. You'll know it. You'll say to yourself: That's a funny name for a pub. Go right there. Up a bit of a hill. Lots of turnings off, but don't take any of them. Just when you think you've come too far, because there's nothing in sight, go a little bit further. The road bends round and there it is.'

'That's Seaview Gardens?'

He laughed again. 'You can see the sea all right. Good travelling, ladies.'

We made certain we hadn't been followed. Nobody else had got off the train and the cyclist had ridden off in the opposite direction to us.

'We can relax, Bernie. Take in the sea air.'

The air wasn't exactly pleasant. Rotting weed and the diesel smell of the docks. It was no easy task to get the other side of them. They gouged a deep slash in the coastline. Once upon a time it must have been a river mouth. It had been widened and deepened with new concrete sides. Half a mile inland we found a bridge.

'Oh, no, there must be another way round.'

Bernie looked at me. 'Whatsamatter? You've gone a funny colour.'

'It's all right. I'll get over it. It's just that bridges make me feel a bit ill.'

I saw something in her face then, a sort of rage of disappointment like a child who's pulled the false beard off Santa. You never know until it's over how hooked you can become on adulation, while all the while protesting otherwise.

'Come on,' I said irritably, then tried to turn it into a joke. 'True courage, Grasshopper, lies not in fearlessness but in the facing of fear. Are you ready?' Then I waved my arms orientally.

She shrugged and followed me.

Huge lorries thundered past us. I didn't look down. We clung to the foot-wide kerb and waited as they passed. Stepped on a few paces, waited, stepped. It was slow but we got to the other side.

'See?' I said, collapsing on to the dusty grass. 'Not so bad.'

There was a road that cut in overland. I thought we ought to keep to the shore so we wouldn't get lost. The shore road dribbled out into a cobbled square. Boats were moored along the water's edge. They had the salt-bleached, tarry look of working boats. The smell was strong but I couldn't see any fish. Too late in the day.

A building blocked our way, a pub of old grey stone that seemed to rise from the water like a natural feature. It couldn't be the white pub? The Ship. You could confuse grey for white as in the 'white cliffs of Dover', but by no stretch of the imagination could the Ship be a funny name for a pub planted right on the edge of the sea.

We went round it. Out back were half a dozen tables and benches. I considered stopping for a drink. All the tables were occupied by men with leathery skin and pale hair, dressed in shades of blue. They looked at us slowly, as you would a cloud. Not hostile, but their faded blue eyes had that closeness of men who work together and distrust outsiders. One got up and followed us.

We walked on. Beyond the fishing-boat moorings was a fenced-off yachting marina. The sea had been sectioned into neat rectangles, on which bobbed the sleek white toys of the rich. I was surprised at how small most of them were, but the perfect polished wood and the gleaming hulls spelt money, money, money. I was parched but I didn't give a second glance to the glass-fronted club-house.

'The next café we come to, Bernie, we'll have a sit-down. If I'd have known it was this far I'd have got a cab.'

'I thought you said cabs weren't safe.'

We'd lost the man from the Ship at the marina.

'That was just detective nonsense. If we were being followed even I would have noticed on this tortuous route.'

We must have been walking an hour before we saw the café. What passed for the beach was a little crescent of sand, rapidly eaten by the rising tide. People were picking up their towels and wet children and bundling them over the sea wall. Further along was a larger area of grey pebbles. Some were spreading themselves there. A string of bathers dried themselves off along a low wall. The dry ones were crowding into the café.

The Anchor Café was where the main road (which we'd turned off by the dock) rejoined the coast. We'd come the long way round and we'd come too far.

The quick-driers already had plates in front of them: of battered fish and chips; sausage, beans and chips; egg and chips; steaming mugs of tea. The chips were those big, irregular, golden chunks of real old potatoes, fried that minute in the kitchen. I could hear the fat bubbling and hissing. A woman with a wet red face was scooping them out on to plates as soon as they were done.

Bernie gaped. 'Chips.'

'We'll never get served.'

Even as we stood there, twenty more people lined up in front of the counter. There were people with plates everywhere, not just at the tables, on the wall, sitting in the gravelly yard, perched along the kerb.

'Come on, Bernie. Let's find the pub with the funny name.'

She glared at me.

A hundred yards back along the main road, on a corner, sat the big white pub. It was called the Cumbernauld, but there was no mistaking it. There was a road sign opposite. It pointed up, to the right: 'Sports Centre and Back Cliff'.

There was no reason now to ask why he hadn't said follow the signs for the Sports Centre.

'Let's have a drink, Bernie.'

'Back Cliff. I think I know where we are.'

The pub sign was a caveman holding up a map on an animal skin. What association that had with Cumbernauld I couldn't imagine. I suppose that's why it stuck in the railman's mind.

'A pint of best bitter and a half of shandy.'

'Is that for the child?'

'She's eighteen. She can drink what she likes.'

'Girl, is it? Not in my bar.'

'It's all right. I'll just have a lemonade,' Bernie whispered. 'This is always happening to me.'

'I said she's eighteen.'

'And I said I'm not serving her alcohol. You can drink it outside. What kind of a woman are you?'

'I just want lemonade,' Bernie said loudly.

It was no punishment drinking outside. A long bench ran the length of the side wall. There were big tubs of flowers and hanging baskets. You could hear, but not see, the sea.

'What was that about?' I asked Bernie.

'You don't know? Why do you think we all come to London?'

The 'bit of a hill' seemed to go on for ever. I could tell Bernie blamed me. Several times we thought we must have come too far. But there was always another road off, another row of neat orange bungalows. They couldn't be for elderly people. The climb would kill them.

'I'm sure there's a short-cut,' said Bernie. 'Along the cliff.'

'Oh no, we don't.'

We overtook a woman leaning on a pushchair. It seemed

as if it was dragging her up the hill. The baby slept on unperturbed. A little bus passed us.

'Shit. Why didn't he tell us there was a bus?'

'How much further? I'm starving.'

'We'll just walk up to the next bus stop.'

I hadn't noticed any, but I hadn't been looking.

'She was always baking cakes, that's what Billie said. Cakes and buns and muffins.'

The hill levelled out. We rounded a bend into wild country, brambles and long overgrown hedges spilled across the footpath.

'There's the sea.'

We must have cut across a headland. The sea was on the opposite side to where it was from the Anchor Café. The road rose up again to our right. To the left a path snaked to the naked cliff edge, with nothing but a fragile wire between us and a hundred-foot drop. It wasn't quite sheer. There were bits of bushes and lumps of sea grass spotted over the rock face, but it wasn't a way you'd choose without ropes and pitons.

'Don't even think of it,' I warned Bernie.

I had stopped with my back to the road, leaning on a concrete fence post to catch my breath. I heard the car. A powerful engine. It was coping quietly with the steep gradient.

'It's him!' Bernie shrieked, and scuttled off down the cliff path.

'Bernie! No.'

By the time I'd turned, the car was a blot cresting the hill, dark against the horns of the noon sun.

Bernie. Not the cliff.

the cliff

The cliff. It's all happening again.

I am standing in a high place, the horizon far below me. My arm rests on grey stone. It is my job to watch. Watch them falling like dolls, over and over. Over and over down to a whispering tissue-paper sea.

My hand holds tight to the rail. I lean. Over and over. Watch the falling dolls. One and another. Over the whispering paper. Ocean as grey as ribbons.

I freeze. Reaching. The boy leached grey as paper. Rolls over and over. Waving like ribbons, weightless. My job is to watch, not catch. Slow as dolls they go over. Reaching like ribbons.

Over and over. I dream this. Over and over.

'I think you need to see a doctor.'

People think of madness as everything falling apart. This is worse. Much worse. Everything crowding together, merging. Churning like washing in a machine. All the colours running. Past present future all stretched and jostled to a chewing-gum grey glue. Faces melting to masks, masks molted to latex. Colour leaching away. To grey. Grey.

The sky is grey and empty. But for the whistling. The sea is grey. Between them only a thin grey wire.

In the dream I am always frozen. Still. Rigid. I reach my hand to the wire. It burns my fingers with its freezing presence. It is real.

174

I must walk. I cannot move my eyes. If I hold the wire at arm's length I can edge along the path. There is something I must do. Stop them. Save them. This time.

I can move. My legs are rock, rooted to the cliff face. It takes all my strength to lift them. My stomach is light, flutters like a ribbon in the wind. Inch by inch I am going forward. I raise my eyes. I can see Bernie bobbing ahead of me, pulling herself up by handfuls of scrunchy grass.

The path I can manage, but no climbing. I try to call to her. Don't. Take care. Don't fall. She is above and ahead now. Laughing. Small stones fly from her scrambling boots. The whole rock face is loose, echoing.

I am walking now, more confident. Fingers barely grazing the wire for reassurance. What did I say, Grasshopper? Face the fear and it is conquered. I breathe easy for the first time. Easy. Nothing to it. Face the fear. Walk. Confident. Walk and . . .

Dead. Stop. Nothing. No path. No . . . Nothing.

The wire curls, twanging loose in the wind. Stomach whips and curls. The sea is very close, sneering.

A piece of cliff face has broken off and tumbled into the sea. The broken bits jag at the grey rolling silk. The rock is bare, almost smooth, a long concave gouge like a scoop taken from a block of wet clay.

This is why Bernie was climbing. Is climbing. Up, far ahead. Her squat body foreshortened, jointless like a rag doll. A boy doll in her baby butch clothes. She turns to wave. Calls. Her voice lost in the wind. Don't. Hang on with both hands. It's dangerous. Not another one. Please. Stay there. I'm coming for you.

And I realize the decision is already made. I am climbing. As if with some dream knowledge, my hands are already clutching the scaly stems of bushes. My feet scrape and dig and lodge firm. My face is pressed to the grey-brown dirt. Dust on my eyelids. My palms are pierced by silvery spines. Grasp, dig, push.

No one will ever believe this. Carole would ... My stomach spins. Beware over-confidence. Grip tight. Keep your eyes up. Look at Bernie. Scrunch, haul, scramble. Clear your mind of everything but the climb. The top of the scoop is in sight. Bernie has gained the other side. Not exactly a path but a gentler slope. A few more heaves.

Dust and sweat sting my eyes. I twist my face to wipe it on my outstretched arms. I blink.

Bernie's gone. Disappeared. She must have fallen. I lean out from the rock for a better view. The sea seethes below me. The rock face is empty. A fall of small stones from above. Bernie?

What's he doing here? Everything slows down. Stomach slips. Hands open. Feet lose their hold. I am scraping, sliding down. My clothes snag on branches but nothing holds me. My head falls back. Crack ...

I am sprawled across a big bush or a small tree. The sun is hot on my face. Burning. The skin is damp and gritty. My father is leaning over me. He's very far away. Far away as the sun. I can barely see him. I squint my eyes into the sun. There he is, at the top of the cliff, leaning over, looking for me.

'I'm here,' I call. It comes out as a thin squeak. Not loud enough to be heard over the pounding of the sea and the rattling of the wind in the dry leaves.

My father's here. He didn't fall. Then I see the boy clambering down over the rocks. It hasn't happened yet. Any minute the boy will fall, and my father after him. I couldn't stop it. Big grey tears fill my vision.

She's leaning over me. 'You're crying. Are you hurt?'

'You disappeared,' I wail.

My face is soaked with tears and stinging. She uses her hankie like a washcloth, wipes the muck away. Roughly.

'I was hiding,' she says.

'You bitch. You know I'm scared of heights. You know about the boy and . . . How could you? You said you loved me.' The rest is sobbing.

Huge gouging sobs that tear the insides out of me. 'Oh, Carole, how could you?'

Then those blood-freezing words. 'I think you need to see a doctor.'

But this time she doesn't say them. She folds me in her arms and covers my face with kisses. 'I do love you. I wouldn't do anything to scare you. I just had to hide.'

I let myself be wrapped in her sweet earthy smell.

'Who's Carole?'

We were sitting on a dusty slope under a wind-twisted tree. I didn't know how she got me down from there. I must have fallen across the diagonal slash in the rock face, for now we were on the other side, lower down. I could see the continuation of the path with its shining wire, just above the tree.

'You called me Carole.'

I patted Bernie's hand. 'You're too good to be Carole. She was the one I told you about. We went for a picnic on Beachy Head. She had this way of twisting her wedding ring.'

I looked down at Bernie's innocent, grubby fingers. 'She was always supposed to be leaving her husband. Next week. Next year. The wedding ring was her way of keeping me in my place. I must have said something to make her angry. She went to the edge and disappeared.'

Bernie gasped.

'It's a famous suicide spot. Lovers' leap. I thought . . .
She reappeared laughing. I couldn't stop crying.'

'Bitch,' breathed Bernie. 'And she knew you were . . . ?'

'I couldn't stop crying for days. Literally. It was like a tap
jammed on. She said I needed to see a doctor. Of course, I
agreed. Nobody wants to be that miserable.'

Bernie looked down at her scarred wrists. 'No. So they
locked you up?'

'Yes. They never did agree on why. I had a different
diagnosis every day. They tried out all their wonder drugs
on me. I think I got sane when I got really angry.'

'I would have killed her.'

'Exactly. That's when they started me on the really heavy-
duty stuff. I got out eventually, but I'd learned a few things.'

It looked like I was unlearning them. I took my hand
away from Bernie's. There you go, trusting people again,
making yourself vulnerable.

'And you thought I was doing the same thing?' Bernie
asked eagerly, misreading my body language. 'I wouldn't do
that, scare you for a laugh. I had to hide. I saw him. The
man in the black car.'

'Oh, yes?' I got up, slapped the dust off my clothes. 'Just
like I saw my father, who's been dead twenty-nine years,
and the boy. My excuse is I banged my head, what's yours?'

She opened her mouth but didn't say anything, just
scowled down at her boots.

'Thank you for rescuing me, but you wouldn't need to
have done if you hadn't gone haring across these cliffs in the
first place. Come on, let's find Billie.'

We kept to the path from then on, and I never let Bernie
out of my sight. As we rounded the final turn, there before
us, a dozen yards from the end of the cliff path, was Seaview
Gardens.

We counted off the houses down the street. Number fifteen didn't look any different from any of the others. There was a small front garden, then a patch of grass at the side which ran into the back. I knocked at the front door.

It was opened by a small woman about ten years my senior. She held her head at an odd perky angle and shook back her hair nervously. It had faded, like upholstery bleached by sunlight, from red to a gingery pink. It was tied, but loosely, with a scrap of pale yellow seam binding.

'Hello, we're friends of Billie. May we come in?'

She shook her head. 'There's no Billie here.'

gender benders

'I don't know no Billie.'

Something in her stance, the ordinary fadedness of her, convinced me. There was nothing to connect her with dismembered bodies, runaway teenagers, and Soho sleaze.

I heard a creaking above the distant whisper of the sea. A girl with blonde ringlets was sitting on a swing at the back. Her pale head came into view by the side of the house, then disappeared.

How had we ended up in this desolately normal place? I looked at Bernie. She was still scowling down at the grass. Bernie had dragged me here. Bernie had led me to risk my neck and my sanity on the cliff top.

'Well, I'm sorry to have troubled you. My young friend must have made a mistake. I'll have a little talk with her later.'

'I'm sorry you've come all this way for nothing. Like I told your friend, there's no boys here, no one called Billie.'

Bernie's head came up. 'Friend?'

'The social worker. Big chap. I thought you were together.'

Bernie's eyes glittered with triumph. I kicked her.

'Oh, him!' I laughed. 'No, we're not from Social Services. He came in a car? We had to walk up from the station. How long ago was he here?'

'You missed him by minutes. I thought it was you he was

looking for on the cliff. Shame, you could have had a lift back. You all being up from London, like.'

'Yes, it is a shame. Especially since my young friend took us up the quick way by the cliffs. You know what young people are. I wonder, would it be terribly rude to ask if we might come in for a bit? A glass of water. I'm rather parched.'

'I don't know. You're not social workers then? What do you do?'

'Well,' I said. Should I tell the truth? What truth?

Bernie grinned. 'Not much. She's just out of a mental hospital, and I sleep on the streets.'

'I suppose you better come in. You'll be wanting something to eat.'

She led us into a lounge. The furniture was indeed sun-bleached, but pale blue rather than red. I jumped at her offer, and asked if I might use the bathroom to clean myself up.

I looked terrible. My face was scratched and tanned with rubbed-in clay. What sort of a woman let someone looking like me into her neat home? The bathroom was small but spotless, with an avocado bath and tiles, and gold taps. There was something going on here I didn't understand.

The tea came in large but delicate bone china cups. The pattern was 'Old Rose'. A second trip to the kitchen produced a plate with three different kinds of cake.

'You're in luck. I've been baking.'

Her smile was brittle, false. She rubbed just the tips of her fingers together; they rustled like dry corn.

'I suppose you do a lot more baking, with children,' I ventured.

'Children?'

'I thought we saw someone.'

'Oh, in the garden? That's my niece, Daphne.' She put her head on one side.

'Can we see her?' asked Bernie.

The smile seemed to implode. 'I suppose so. Now?'

Bernie was tucking into the homemade walnut cake. 'Umhm.' She nodded, mouth full.

The woman ran her thin fingers through the top of her hair, replaced a grip. 'OK.' It was almost a whisper.

Daphne stood in the doorway, twisting the lap of her frock in her fingers. It was a flouncy, girly, blue and white creation that was either too young or too old for her. With the fat curls, it made her look as if she'd just stepped off the Yellow Brick Road.

Bernie was looking at her strangely.

'I think,' she said, putting down her plate of cake, 'that this is a painted hussy.'

It all happened at once. Bernie jumped up. They were yelling and circling and hugging like wrestlers, and punching arms. All noise and tangle. It took a while to hear what they were shouting.

'Gender bender!'

They were laughing and hanging off each other. Bernie grabbed a handful of blonde curls. I'd never seen her like this. The other's face was wet and flushed and, I now saw, oddly familiar.

'Boss, meet my friend Billie.'

burgers

Inspector Tennyson seemed to be expecting my call. We agreed to meet in a burger bar. It was not my choice of venue.

We'd gone over it a dozen times. Nothing could go wrong. We'd all be safe, especially Billie. I had a signed and witnessed statement from him which I posted to myself recorded delivery at my office address. I told Tennyson if I didn't make the meeting to look out for it.

'Don't you think that's a trifle melodramatic, Miss Aachen?'

'You don't know what's in it.'

'I could make a fair guess.'

'Shall we wait till the meeting?'

We all caught different trains. That was part of the plan. Billie's was a return ticket. He intended staying with his foster mother. Her husband had died eighteen months ago. She'd never been able to get a message to Billie.

'It's a terrible thing to say, with her so recently dead, but I'm glad it's turned out like this. He'd never have come back except he was feared for his life. He hated my husband, see. Something about dressing in girl's clothes. He was a hard man, and he didn't like nothing irregular. Always picking at the lad he was. Then something happened and my Billie ran away for the last time.'

She was in her kitchen telling me this, collecting up the

ingredients for another batch of cakes. Whipping up a batter was her way of dealing with strong emotion. I've seen worse.

'He's not had a lot of good things in his life. That woman was like a mother to him in her way. But, how do I say this? Her dying like that, it made him see that it's a dangerous place, that London. Maybe when he's older. He can always go and see her, the young girl, when she's got her flat. It's funny them. Like something got switched at birth.'

From the way she beat I thought it was going to be a very light sponge.

It was evening when I caught the train. The station seemed deserted. Even my friendly guide had disappeared. Maybe Tennyson was right about the melodrama.

I had other reasons for seeking an empty carriage. I wanted to be alone. I didn't think I was in any physical danger, but ever since Billie gave me his statement I felt the whole world turning round me. A lurch of perspective, as when you lean back and look at the sky from a swing and it seems that you are the only still spot in a heaving universe.

At some level I had always known. That was the explanation for the sense of it all being preordained, of us being mere dancers going through prescribed steps. I could not own it consciously, for that would mean my whole universe shifting on its axis.

On the cliff, I had seen what I'd seen. Only my mind kept forcing the present into the mould of the past. Time, like gender, is more fluid than we think. But we will keep trying to fix it, as if our sanity depended on it.

The whole journey was touched with foreboding. The uncanny, someone had said, was but the return of the repressed. I was losing my grip: I couldn't remember the source of my quotes. This time, I thought, it won't hold. Everything will come flooding through.

Evian flitted through my brain. I wondered if she ever dreamt she was a man again and woke up screaming. Would it feel like loss? A kind of death?

Christine Deerhart said I would have to face my own demons. She couldn't force me. What would it feel like if I released the dammed-up waters? Would I lose my power? Maybe it would feel like kissing a dry leaf, from which all the vitality had evaporated.

I kept seeing my face reflected back from the dark in different windows, sometimes strangely doubled so it seemed I was peering over my own shoulder. I felt my appointment with the policeman was like going to meet death.

In the event, the burger bar was crowded and there didn't seem any place on the red and yellow surfaces for that visitor. Tennyson was already there. I ordered a large shake, a double cheeseburger and chips, and a cup of tea for myself. He was half-way through an apple pie.

'Well, here we are, Miss Aachen.'

He smiled and there was something in the gaunt features that made me want to cry. He reminded me of my father, though there wasn't any physical likeness. Wouldn't it all have been so much easier if there had?

I sensed a great well of sympathy, which could never be drained. How did he cope with hate? There must be so much of it swirling round his feet. It is rare to find such obvious incorruptibility. Yet he must be responsible for locking away young men, depriving them for years of their liberty. Had he ever convicted an innocent person, concocted evidence? Get a grip, H.

He was a small man with large hands; you could imagine them spread to cradle a baby. 'Do you have any children?'

'That's an odd question, Miss Aachen.' He smiled an

infinitely sad smile. 'If I asked that of a woman, you'd probably think me sexist.'

'*Touché*. Inspector, you know why I wanted to see you.'

On cue, Billie slid in beside me and immediately started on the cheeseburger. He was still in his Daphne mode.

'It's all in the statement, but I thought you'd like to hear it directly from the witness.'

He nodded.

'All right, Billie. Tell the Inspector about the last time you saw Rusty. That's Rosetta Stirling, the woman in question.'

He took another gulp of cheeseburger. 'Well, I was waiting on the corner to meet her. It's just after midnight. We always went for something to eat in her break. She was sort of like a mother to me.'

I was watching Tennyson's face carefully. It was impassive.

'She sees me and she's just running over to me. She can't run very well because she's got these stupid shoes on, and all that junk she wears for work. She's got a mac on but it's not done up, so you can see it all when she runs. Before she gets to me, a car pulls up. He says something to her and she says something back.'

Tennyson didn't say anything, so I asked, 'Could you hear what they said?'

Billie shook the fat curls. 'No. But what I thought then was: it's a punter and she don't want to.'

'That's just what you thought. How old are you, Billie?' I felt like a trial judge.

'Fifteen.'

'Go on.'

All this time Tennyson moved not a muscle.

'Then he pulls her into the car. She didn't want to go, but she sort of shrugs and waves to me. Like: Go on, I'm going to be busy here, sort of thing.'

186

'OK, Billie. Did you get to see his face?'

'Yes.'

'Did you recognize him?'

'Yes, I seen him around a lot. Round the clubs.'

I had my eyes fixed on Tennyson. 'Can you tell me who he was, Billie?'

'Detective Sergeant Scott. It was no mistaking him.'

the dam bursts

Tennyson's eyebrows lifted a fraction, then dropped back. His eyelids did the same. It was as if a tiny cloud had passed over and was gone. 'He's resigned.'

I felt as if a globe of silence had descended over us and blocked out all the noise of the burger bar.

'I believe him when he says it was an accident.'

My mouth tasted brackish. I rinsed it out with some of the cold tea. 'How long have you known?'

'Known? He'd been acting strangely ever since it happened. I suspected something but I didn't know what. Then, you identified the car. I called him into the office. He denied it at first, but I knew.'

'The black car?'

'You frightened him, your persistence. That's why he pulled you in in the first place, to find out what you knew. You know what he said to me? That you were always one jump ahead of him. You even got to the boy first.'

I didn't know whether to laugh or cry. 'I didn't, in fact. But maybe it's not getting there first, but knowing you've got there, that's important. Why did you never let on? What's going to happen now?'

'He's not a bad lad. Working here did for him, all the filth, temptation . . .'

'I can't believe I'm hearing this. What about what he did to Rusty, chopping her up?'

'That was after she was dead.'

'And that makes it better I suppose?' I was screaming, but I still felt nobody could hear.

'Think about it, Miss Aachen.'

'What's going to happen to him – Scott?'

'We wouldn't have had a case.'

'You mean: nothing. He gets away with it.' Scot-free was what came into my mind. There was a malignancy about how their names lent themselves to puns.

'He's lost his job. His career prospects are blighted. The fact that we know, the statement you've got, is a guarantee against anything like it happening again. We're not going to charge him. So, yes, if you like, he's getting away with it.'

'Do you think that's right?'

'It's not my decision. We wouldn't make it stick in a court of law. My superiors aren't in the business of losing murder trials.'

'It's not fair,' I wailed.

'What did you expect, Miss Aachen? That he take himself off with his old service revolver and do the decent thing? People don't do the decent thing. This isn't Kipling.'

I hardly heard his last words. There came a great wet rushing. Howling of a burst dam. 'No, no, it's not fair. He can't be. No, no, no.'

It went on and on. The circle of silence widened. Our little table was like an island amid the rising waters. No one came near.

When it eventually subsided, Tennyson was on my side of the table with his arm round my shoulder. 'It's all right, Haydon. It's not fair. It's all right.'

He put a cup of tea in my hand. The polystyrene cup crumpled and the tea ran down my fingers.

'Oh dear, I've made a bit of a show.'

'They're used to it,' he said gently.

'Just one more mad woman in a tacky café. Did I tell you about my father, Inspector? He was a police officer. He was also a manic depressive. That's one of the few mental illnesses they've established as hereditary.'

'That doesn't mean anything. It doesn't mean you—'

'There was a boy. When I was seven. You were wrong, Inspector, about nobody doing the decent thing. The boy died and my father threw himself off a railway bridge on to an oncoming train. He couldn't bear the shame of it.'

Tennyson didn't say anything. He waited, as if that wasn't the end of the story.

'I've never told anybody else. Even my mother and I don't speak about it. I've just carried it around for twenty-nine years.'

'It was pre-Wolfenden.'

'He'd reported but the law hadn't changed. I don't suppose it applies to policemen, anyway.'

He looked down at his big hands. H., you are so slow. 'Not in any way that matters. The gay policeman is a cabaret joke,' he said, 'sadly.'

'I don't suppose he was responsible for that boy's death, even accidentally. He was just terrified that it would come out about the relationship. It's a terrible way to go. I saw a television programme about it once. With fast Intercity trains, limbs can get sliced off and fly out in different directions. I don't suppose they had those sort of trains then.'

'What are you going to do, Haydon?'

'Me? I feel as though I've been reprieved from a life sentence. All these years I've gone around believing . . . It sounds stupid.'

190

'He had to be guilty because otherwise why did he have to die?'

'Worse than that. That I was a carrier, that it was contagious this connection between love and death and punishment. That I mustn't let myself, ever.'

'And now you've been cleared.'

'Yes. What will I do? I think I'll have to go to Dorking and look up Forster's gay policeman. Amongst other things.' No need to spill all my secrets.

I picked up my jacket and searched the refuse-strewn table.

'If you're looking for your purse, I think you'll find it in the ladies', empty.'

'He didn't?'

'What a world, Miss Aachen. Where are all the good men gone? And innocent children?'

Other Vista crime titles include:

Kick Back Val McDermid   0 575 60007 1

Dead Beat Val McDermid   0 575 60002 0

Paint it Black Mark Timlin   0 575 60014 4

Falconer's Judgement Ian Morson   0 575 60004 7

Falconer's Crusade Ian Morson   0 575 60079 9

The Death Prayer David Bowker   0 575 60028 4

Poet in the Gutter John Baker   0 575 60045 4

Significant Others Robert Richardson   0 575 60049 7

Sharman and Other Filth Mark Timlin   0 575 60101 9

Invitation to a Funeral Molly Brown   0 575 60036 5

Sicken and So Die Simon Brett   0 575 60048 9

The Curious Eat Themselves John Straley   0 575 60135 3

Flashback Jim Lusby   0 575 60066 7

Find My Way Home Mark Timlin   0 575 60176 0

Falconer and the Face of God Ian Morson   0 575 60063 2

Big Italy Timothy Williams   0 575 60018 7

Fast Road to Nowhere Joe Canzius   0 575 60104 3

The Trapdoor Andrew Klavan   0 575 60230 9